TOURNAMENT
FUGEE

TOURNAMENT FUGEE

Dirk McLean

James Lorimer & Company Ltd., Publishers
Toronto

Copyright © 2017 by Dirk McLean
Some characters appearing in this book are copyright © David Starr.
Published in Canada in 2017. Published in the United States in 2018.

All rights reserved. No part of this book may be reproduced or transmitted in
any form or by any means, electronic or mechanical, including photocopying,
or by any information storage or retrieval system, without permission in
writing from the publisher.

James Lorimer & Company Ltd., Publishers acknowledges the support of
the Ontario Arts Council (OAC), an agency of the Government of Ontario,
which in 2015-16 funded 1,676 individual artists and 1,125 organizations in
209 communities across Ontario for a total of $50.5 million. We acknowledge
the support of the Canada Council for the Arts, which last year invested $153
million to bring the arts to Canadians throughout the country. This project
has been made possible in part by the Government of Canada and with the
support of the Ontario Media Development Corporation.

Cover design: Shabnam Safari
Cover image: iStock

Library and Archives Canada Cataloguing in Publication

McLean, Dirk, 1956-, author
    Tournament fugee / Dirk McLean.

Issued in print and electronic formats.
ISBN 978-1-4594-1225-5 (softcover).--ISBN 978-1-4594-1227-9 (EPUB)

    I. Title.

PS8575.L3894T68 2017   jC813'.54   C2017-903301-8
                                            C2017-903302-6

Published by: Distributed in Canada by: Distributed in the US by:
James Lorimer &   Formac Lorimer Books   Lerner Publisher Services
Company Ltd., Publishers   5502 Atlantic Street   1251 Washington Ave. N.
117 Peter Street, Suite 304   Halifax, NS, Canada   Minneapolis, MN, USA
Toronto, ON, Canada   B3H 1G4   55401
M5V 0M3   www.lernerbooks.com
www.lorimer.ca

Manufactured by Friesens Corporation in Altona, Manitoba,
Canada in July 2017.
Job #234939

For Renée, Jessica and Melissa.
And my mother, Jacqueline.

"People in this world don't know
how other people does affect their lives."

Sam Selvon, The Lonely Londoners

Contents

PROLOGUE
Kicking the Ball

Victor tucked his beat-up soccer ball under his arm and jumped off the back of the truck. He joined his family gathered at the side of the road. He had to rescue his prized possession.

The truck sped away, leaving them at the crossroads.

"How far are we from the border, Grampa?" Victor asked.

Grampa Bayazid scratched his grey beard and peered into the distance. Then he pointed along the highway.

"About twenty kilometres, if it is Allah's will," he said. "Victor, you have strong legs to kick that ball. Maybe we skip a mile, yes," he chuckled.

Victor grinned. He was used to Grampa's humour. He knew that Grampa would tell stories along the way to make the journey seem shorter.

They set off under the mid-morning sun. Ahead of Victor and Grampa were Victor's mom, dad and his six-year-old brother Gabriel. They all had as many of their belongings as they could carry.

Ten-year-old Victor knew that this was not an ordinary family outing. With each step forward they were leaving the land of their birth, the Syria they loved and may never see again. By the next morning they would be in Lebanon, another country. They would become the same as those who had already fled ahead to freedom. It was a word whispered in households across the land — refugees.

A few hours later, with the sun high in the cloudless sky, the Bayazid family was marching along the paved highway. The oncoming vehicles were few and far between. Victor bounced his soccer ball. He loved the sound of it striking the hardened earth beside the road. He was careful not to bounce it on a pebble. He didn't want it to roll onto the highway away from him.

They had passed other families along the way. Others had suddenly appeared from the sides of the road, having camped the night before. Victor knew there were many families behind them fleeing the danger in Syria. He imagined he was a hawk high above, watching the people crawl like ants toward a giant pomegranate lying in the distance. The fruit was freedom, and its ripe seeds could feed millions.

Grampa walked beside Victor but closer to the highway, protecting him.

"Victor," Grampa said, "your mother and father are responsible for you and Gabriel. That is true no matter what changes happen in your lives. And you are responsible for Gabriel. You understand?"

"Yes, Grampa." Victor nodded.

"You are separated by four years. You'll be able to teach him a lot, for you have your lives ahead of you."

"You mean like soccer?"

"Yes, that," Grampa chuckled. "But much, much more."

The border between Syria and Lebanon was friendly. Grampa had a solid plan about where they should cross. He had been to Lebanon many times in his life. There he had made lifelong friends who would help his family.

They came across a clearing right beside the highway. Victor could see that people had camped there. There was a clump of ashes where a fire had kept them warm during the cold night in the desert wilderness.

Grampa checked his watch.

"What time is it, Grampa?" Victor asked.

"Look at the sun. It's directly above us. Haven't I taught you how to read the sun, the wind, the clouds and the stars?" he scolded in a joking manner.

"Not yet, Grampa."

"Then I am not being a responsible grampa," he said, pointing to the sun. "It's almost noon. We eat. Lessons after lunch."

The Bayazid family unrolled thin prayer mats and knelt facing east. They said the midday prayer, led by Grampa. Then they sat and shared a meal of flat bread, olives, dried dates and almonds. They sipped only enough water to help the food go down to their stomachs.

"Family," Grampa said, looking around at each of them. "There's nothing more important than family."

While the adults rested, Victor and Gabriel kicked the soccer ball to each other. Victor began thinking of what Grampa had told him earlier. He began to look forward to all that he would learn in their new life in Lebanon. He thought about all that he would share with Gabriel.

Gabriel rolled the ball across the orange earth straight toward Victor.

1
Tripped Up

Thirteen-year-old Victor Bayazid stood in front of the goal line, ready to defend a corner kick. His defenders and midfielders jostled with the forwards and midfielders of the North York Engineers. The score was 1–1 and the North York Engineers seemed hungry to break that tie against Victor's Scarborough Tigers. It was a must-win match. The winners would advance to the playoff round. The losers — well, that would be the end of their indoor-league season.

The Scarborough Tigers were new to the league. Victor was determined to have them advance and please Coach Jeong-Hough.

"Drew, move a bit to your right!" Victor shouted to his defender. "I can't see clearly."

As Drew Merasty moved over, Victor watched the ball leave the corner spot on his left. It increased in speed as it headed toward his goal. Players were already jumping. Victor knew that he would have to jump higher than everyone else if he was going to catch the ball. Victor had prepared for this play in practice all season. He had thought about it long before, when he decided to be a goalkeeper. He knew more than most the importance of keeping his eyes on the ball no matter what the other team was doing in front of his goal.

Victor bent his knees slightly and sprang up, up, up. He raised his arms high above all the players and willed the spinning ball into his gloved hands. When it was safely there, Victor hugged the ball into his chest for extra security. He cradled it like it was the most precious thing in the world. And at that moment, it was. His feet landed back on earth. Actually, it was the green artificial turf of the field. He knew without looking that he had landed in front of his goal line. It was a good goalkeeper's save.

Then Victor felt something strange. A foot struck his left heel, hard. In a play like a corner kick, with players bunched in front of the goal, Victor had often felt someone land on his cleat. He had even been kicked on his shin. Never before had he felt anything behind his leg.

In an instant Victor's left leg was up. He felt his body falling backwards. He could not stop himself. As his back hit the turf the ball flew out of his hands behind him. Victor heard a sound that seemed to come from far away. As it got closer, and louder, he recognized the ref's whistle. Victor knew that he was lying behind the goal line.

Tripped Up

Where is the ball?

Victor rolled over and saw the ball nestled against the back of the net.

As Drew helped Victor to his feet, he saw the Engineers celebrating.

"Did you see that?" Victor asked Drew.

"You caught the ball, Victor," Drew replied. "And then you fell. You scored on your own goal, man."

"I didn't," Victor protested. "I was tripped."

Victor ran over to where Coach Jeong-Hough stood on the sideline. "Didn't you see, Coach?" he asked.

Coach Jeong-Hough shook her head.

Victor turned to Raymond Park, their captain. "Raymond, somebody tripped me."

"You fell, Victor. It happens," Coach Jeong-Hough said with a shrug. "We still have twelve minutes to score two goals and win this match."

Victor looked over at Ozzie. Ozzie was his friend and team co-goalkeeper who had played the first half. Ozzie, too, shook his head.

The ref came over to Victor. "Time to take your place," he ordered.

Something inside Victor snapped. He felt that no one was supporting him. He felt like he had no *place* to take, not anymore. "Ozzie, you take my place," he said. "I'm done."

Then Victor did something he never thought he would do. He walked off the field.

Victor sat in the change room. He was dressed in street clothes with his winter coat on his lap. Voices still echoed in his head.

"What the hell are you doing?" midfielder Foster asked.

"Victor, you come back here!" Coach Jeong-Hough yelled.

"Stop, man, that's crazy!" said Nathan in his Jamaican accent.

"You're gonna be suspended!" Raymond shouted.

Victor thought back to the moment he felt the leg on his heel. In his mind he scanned the faces of the North York Engineers around the goal. One face stood out, and it was wearing a sneer. Randy Harris. Randy had once called Victor a name when the Tigers played against them before. Victor knew that Randy was the one who tripped him. He also knew there was no way he could ever prove it.

When Victor's team returned to the change room, the way they straggled in told the story. They had lost. Victor thought of leaving right away. Yet something inside him said that if he did, things would be worse on the minibus home. He decided to look each of his teammates in the eye as their abuse started.

"Never thought you'd be a quitter, Victor."

"Don't come begging for a spot next season."

"Thanks for screwing up our season."

"We could have made the playoffs if you weren't so clumsy."

"You should never have been on this team, *boy*."

Others stared at Victor without saying a word. He kept his gaze on them. It surprised him how easily some of them turned against him. But he wasn't going to show them how much that hurt him.

Ozzie trotted in. He took in the scene and said, "Hey, that's soccer, Victor. Could have gone either way."

"It figures goalkeepers would stand up for each other," said midfielder Dennis Kim.

"Don't get started on me, Dennis!" Ozzie yelled.

"Guys, guys, no fighting," Victor said. He picked up his bag as he stood up. "I'm sorry. That's all."

Walking out of the change room, Victor bumped into Coach Jeong-Hough. Victor didn't think he could take it if she was angry with him too. She had played in the World Cup for South Korea, and the fall before she had coached a Grade 7/8 team to become Division Champions. Victor and his coach looked at each other for a few seconds.

"Things happen in soccer, Victor," she started. "How we react, how we behave makes the difference. I expected more from you."

"Sorry, Coach."

"Running away from your team. Disobeying your

coach. Not being responsible. That's unacceptable. I don't think there'll be room for that kind of player next season. I'm truly disappointed."

She walked past him and entered the change room.

Outside, the Saturday afternoon light was starting to fade. Light snow flurries blew around in the cold air. Victor zipped up his coat tighter with his free hand to protect his neck — just like his mom always reminded him. He took a few steps toward the parking lot and the team's minibus. A man wearing a brown suit under an open coat approached Victor. He started speaking in Arabic.

"You are a very talented goalkeeper," he said.

Victor turned around. The man must have been speaking to someone behind him. Seeing no one, he responded, "Are you speaking to me?"

The man grinned and held out a business card. "I only spoke Arabic to get your attention," he said in English. "We'll speak English, yes?"

Victor put his equipment bag on the ground. He took the card and wiped off some snow. What stood out easily was "Mr. Michael Bridge."

"I would like to speak with you and your parents about soccer," the man in the brown suit said. "Please have them call me as soon as it's possible."

Victor nodded. Mr. Bridge held out his hand. Victor shook it. The man's hand was warm — a surprise. Victor slipped the card into his coat pocket and bent down to pick up his bag. When he stood up Mr. Bridge was speaking with Coach Jeong-Hough.

Victor thought of tossing the card. He didn't see any recycling bins close by so he kept the card in his pocket.

Sitting in the minibus, Victor saw Ozzie run out of the soccer complex. His familiar limp was from a childhood accident in Nigeria. Seconds later Victor watched Mr. Bridge approach Muhammad just outside the minibus. Muhammad was Victor and Ozzie's schoolmate at William Hall PS and the top striker on the Tigers.

Victor wondered what Mr. Bridge could be saying to Muhammad, but not to Ozzie. Victor took out the card and held it at an angle so he could read it. Above Mr. Bridge's name it read "Syrian Committee for Thank You Canada Soccer Tournament."

"What's this all about?" he whispered to himself.

2
An Invitation

Victor lived in northeast Scarborough, outside of downtown Toronto. His neighbourhood, Malvern, was home to a mixture of people from all over the world and of all incomes. The Bayazids lived in a two-bedroom apartment in a high-rise. The furnishings were simple with touches of their Syrian background in colourful cushions and throws. The store IKEA had become one of their favourites.

Victor waited until after supper to break the news to his mom and dad. Somewhere Victor had learned that bad news is received better on a full stomach. He had already told them that the Tigers were not in the league playoffs. He made it sound like not a big deal. He said new teams sometimes need a few seasons to strike it big. He reminded his dad that it took Toronto FC ten years before they made it to their first MLS Final.

While clearing the dishes from the dining room, Victor told the full story.

"You should not have been suspended!" Dad roared.

"Don't they have cameras with replays these days?"

"For pro matches," Victor replied. "And sometimes we see things clearer on TV than the refs and lines-people do."

"I'm going to tell that coach what I think," Dad said, picking up his cell phone.

"No need, Dad. The season is over."

Mom joined them and took the phone from Dad's hand. "Many things are not fair, Victor," she said. "Sometimes good things come after bad. We have all learned that."

Victor knew that his mom was referring to leaving Syria in fear for their lives. From Lebanon, they had come to Canada, to Toronto, almost three years earlier as sponsored refugees. And they now had this safe, new life. They were no longer refugees. They were *new* Canadians.

The memories reminded Victor of what it said on Mr. Bridge's card. He dashed to the front closet, fished out the card from his coat pocket and returned to the dining room. He handed the card to his mom and dad and explained his meeting with Mr. Bridge. They read the card and turned it over as if they would find the answers to their questions on the back.

"Who is this Michael Bridge?" Dad scowled.

"I don't know anything but what it says here," Victor said.

"He spoke to you in Arabic?" Mom asked. Dad's English was better than Mom's. Victor knew it was true what the Newcomer Centre said — speaking more English at home would help.

Victor nodded.

"It's clear that he had seen you play. Do you remember seeing him at any matches?"

"I — I think so," Victor responded. But he was not sure.

"I have heard nothing about this committee," Dad sneered. "And I listen out for everything about Syrians."

"You don't hear everything about Syrians," Mom teased.

"Okay, okay, almost everything." Dad smiled at Mom.

Victor was glad his parents could still joke with each other. He knew that some of his Syrian friends had parents who were always fighting, even more than they did before coming to Canada.

"You still want to play soccer, Victor?" Dad asked.

"Sure he does," nine-year-old Gabriel piped up.

"Of course, Dad," Victor said at the same time.

"Even after what happened today?"

"Sure."

Dad looked at Mom. She nodded.

"I tell you what we will do," Dad stated. "We will invite this Mr. Michael Bridge to our home. We will look at him face to face. And we will hear what he has to say about himself and this committee."

On Sunday afternoon, while Gabriel was playing with a friend down the hallway, Mr. Bridge was offered a second cup of coffee. Victor watched him sip it like it cost one hundred dollars. He listened politely and watched for any signs of untruth.

Dad was the chief interrogator in the Bayazid Courtroom. Mom was his backup. At times they switched roles. The three adults often switched from English to Arabic and back again. Victor felt like he was watching a bilingual comedy. But he dared not laugh out loud.

Thousands of Syrian refugees had moved to Canada for a new life. Mr. Bridge and other Syrian businesspeople wanted to say thanks to their new country by organizing a soccer tournament. Mr. Bridge, a former Under-14 coach, was going to coach a Greater Toronto Area (or GTA) team. It was one of eight teams from across Canada to play in Vancouver. All the players were Syrian boys.

"And why Under-14 boys?" Dad asked.

"This age group of refugees, thirteen to fourteen, are the most active in soccer across the country," Mr. Bridge replied from the witness stand, known usually as the love seat.

"No girls?" Mom asked.

"Mrs. Bayazid, we did consider girls," Mr. Bridge responded. "We've all had a hard time rounding up boys in the various cities in time for the tournament in about a month. If we had to find girls too, the project would have taken a couple of years. Let me ask you:

would you have said yes any quicker if I was asking you to let a daughter play?"

"We haven't said yes for our son," Mom stated, for the record. "We wish to understand more."

"I have been to several of Victor's matches over the winter. To watch him play," Mr. Bridge confessed.

"So why have you waited until now to talk to us?" Dad asked.

"I promised Coach Jeong-Hough not to poach her players before the season was over."

"Poach? Like eggs?" Mom looked confused. "Explain yourself."

"No, no. I mean I couldn't steal any —"

"You steal?"

"No, no, no. I couldn't make an offer to a player before now," he explained calmly. "Also, the money has only just been put into place for the GTA team. Other cities got funding sooner."

There were more questions and answers. And there were stories exchanged about missing a birthland. Finally, the witness played what Victor would call his trump card.

"Mr. and Mrs. Bayazid, I would like to offer — I would like to invite your son, Victor, to be our goalkeeper. He will travel, all expenses paid, to the tournament in Vancouver."

All expenses paid had not been mentioned. *Definitely the trump card*, Victor decided. He looked at Mom and Dad, who looked at each other. And looked at

An Invitation

Mr. Bridge. Then they all looked at Victor.

"Victor, is this something you would be interested in?" Dad asked. *Vancouver? The edge of the world? For soccer?* Victor beamed and nodded.

"Your mother and I will have to discuss this," Dad said. "Mr. Bridge, how soon do you need our decision?"

"In three days, Mr. Bayazid."

"All right, then."

Victor secretly wished that the Bayazid Court could break for a recess, rather than adjourning for the day.

⚽ ⚽ ⚽

That evening Victor called Ozzie and told him everything. They were in the same grade eight homeroom and had been friends over the past four months. Because of Ozzie and his other passion, reading, Victor's English had improved a lot. But there were still times he struggled to find the right word.

"So, you said yes. But you're not really sure," said Ozzie.

"They were all staring at me. I had to say something. I don't know how I feel about being that far from my family."

"I hear you, Victor. But this is a great chance for a rising soccer star," Ozzie said. "If I was in your place I would not hesitate."

"Then I will offer you honorary Syrian citizenship

to go instead of me."

"That's a generous offer. But being a Nigerian-Trinidadian-Canadian is enough citizenship for me."

"But —"

"It's only ten days," Ozzie reasoned. "Two plane rides. A ton of soccer. You get to be with your people, explore a new city, see mountains *and* the Pacific Ocean. It's sounding better the more I think about it. Maybe I'll go back in time and be born in Syria instead of Nigeria," he joked.

"Mom and Dad still have to give their permission. They're going to check out this committee to make sure I'm not going to be kidnapped and —"

"Wait, wait, wait, you didn't tell me you were the grandson of the *king* of Syria."

"You, Ozzie, read too many books about spies."

Victor felt better after talking to Ozzie. He picked up his sketchpad and sharpened a charcoal pencil. Ms. Tingling, his art teacher, told him to sketch. Not just things around him but also things from his past. That advice was echoed at a Black History Month event at Malvern Public Library by local artists Ras Stone and Charmaine Lurch.

Victor thought of mountains in Syria and he started to sketch.

I hope Mom and Dad don't find something bad about Mr. Bridge or the committee that would stop me from going to Vancouver, he thought.

3
Back to the Bayazid Courtroom

The alarm clock purred. Victor opened his eyes and climbed down from the upper bunk, careful not to wake Gabriel. He stepped into the hallway, closing the bedroom door quietly behind him. He had an urgent need to pee as he staggered to the bathroom. As he reached the door it opened and Dad came out. They nodded to each other. It was their custom at that hour.

Victor stepped into the bathroom in time to remove his pyjama bottoms and release his bladder. He then performed *ablution*, the first of two morning rituals. He washed his hands, rinsed his mouth and cleared his nostrils of mucus. Next he took a fresh facecloth, ran it under warm water and washed his arms and feet. After drying his body, he got dressed. He left the bathroom for the second ritual, called *salat*.

Victor entered the living room, ignoring the pleasant smells of breakfast being cooked by Mom. He unrolled his short prayer rug and laid it on the floor with the top facing east. He stood on the bottom edge and brought his hands together. Closing his eyes, he began salat — a brief prayer to Allah, his God.

This was how Victor began every day. He repeated salat at night before bed. Victor knew that within the next year, when he reached puberty, he would start to do five salats each day.

When he was finished, Victor greeted Mom and Dad. He woke Gabriel and the family sat in the kitchen for a quick breakfast of plain yogurt with honey, eggs, hot cereal, pita bread with goat cheese, date squares and tea.

After breakfast Victor had a quick shower.

"Wear an extra layer, boys. It is minus two degrees this morning," Mom said.

"With a wind chill of minus eighty," Dad added. His imitation of a TV weatherperson made Gabriel giggle.

William Hall PS was only two blocks away. Ozzie had told Victor how the school had been saved from closing almost three years ago. Victor thought about how different it might be if Principal Arsenault had not left her Six Nations school to bring new life to William Hall. Entering homeroom, Victor bumped fists with Ozzie.

"Spring is coming," Ozzie said like it was the biggest announcement of the year. He had been making the same announcement every Monday morning since they had returned to school in January.

They took their seats after a recording of an R&B singer's soulful rendition of "O Canada" played. This was followed by a girl's voice Victor thought he recognized.

"We at William Hall PS acknowledge the Indigenous peoples of Canada who originally lived on the land where our school sits. They looked after it with care and pride. For that we are truly thankful," she said.

Then Principal Arsenault reminded everyone that the next day was Valentine's Day. Victor had planned to ignore that ritual altogether. Of course, there was a girl he had noticed months ago. *Leelah. Yes, it was her beautiful voice that made the announcement.* But there was no way he was going to ask her to be his Valentine. He wished the whole day would simply dissolve. He had other things on his mind.

During lunch Victor sought out Muhammad to find out where he stood on Mr. Bridge's offer. Muhammad told him that his parents had argued after Mr. Bridge left their home.

"Dad said it's too far and I'm too young," Muhammad said almost tearfully.

"And your mom?"

"She surprised me. She wanted me to go. She told my dad that we can't keep being afraid of what might happen to our family."

"Will your dad change his mind?"

"No, it's final. Can't go."

"That sucks."

"Tell me about it. And your parents?" Muhammad asked.

"Dad's playing judge, jury, prosecutor, counsel and private investigator."

Muhammad began to laugh.

"Well, both my parents are. The only role left is star witness," Victor continued. "They want to find out more about the committee. I hope I find out tonight."

⚽ ⚽ ⚽

When Victor got home from school, the jury was still out. Mom and Dad had not made a final decision. There were more family discussions. Mom and Dad had conducted what they called "due diligence," which Victor understood to mean close investigating.

"It's not like I'm going to Antarctica to study how penguins keep warm," he wanted to say.

"The Syrian consulate said that the committee is legitimate," Mom offered. "They confirmed there are seven other committees across Canada. But that just means they haven't yet committed a crime. They could be planning to kidnap one hundred boys and sell them to North Korea or someplace."

"My spies in the community have heard nothing bad," Dad reported. "Then, again, they don't always hear everything."

Geez! They've really become private detectives, Victor thought.

"I can hear what you're thinking, Victor. You are

our child. We have to be careful," said Mom.

Psychic private detectives, now.

"Tomorrow we do more checking. I'll skip lunch," Dad said.

The more Mom and Dad stalled, the more Victor wanted to go to Vancouver.

After supper Dad let Victor and Gabriel watch Arsenal play Barcelona in a Champions League match. Gabriel dozed off early in the second half with Arsenal leading 3–1. Victor watched until the end, picking up goalkeeping tips. He noticed the way the Barcelona goalkeeper punted the ball beyond the half-mark line into Arsenal's territory. Victor made a mental note to practise his punting.

The next night, Mom and Dad shared more of their discoveries with Victor. The main point was why the defendant, Mr. Bridge, had quit coaching Under-14 soccer in Syria. If Mr. Bridge was a quitter, how would he lead a brand new team to Vancouver? Things were not looking good.

Then Dad presented a major piece of evidence to the Bayazid Courtroom.

"It appears that this Mr. Michael Bridge is a devout man," Dad said in his opening statement.

"What does devout mean?" Gabriel asked.

"A devout man is true to his faith," Dad replied. "Mr. Bridge has made the pilgrimage to Mecca in Saudi Arabia. He has travelled to the holy of holies for Muslims."

Dad was smiling. Victor could see that Dad was speaking as defence for Mr. Bridge. That was good. He remembered that Dad had been planning to make the holy journey himself before the troubles started in Syria. Grampa had made the pilgrimage.

"Lady and gentlemen of the jury, I present to you Exhibit A, *El Hajj* Michael Bridge."

Victor knew that if Dad used the title El Hajj, he was willing to trust Mr. Bridge. It could be the tipping point.

But why had he quit coaching?

⚽ ⚽ ⚽

That question was answered the next day when Mr. Bridge arrived with two business partners, Mrs. Isa and Mr. Rahman.

"The authorities were watching me," Mr. Bridge answered. "I knew that my life was in danger. I arranged all my documents and packed one bag. Then I created an argument with the head coach in front of the team before an out-of-town match. I stormed off, saying that I was quitting. I needed witnesses. I was to appear to the authorities for discipline the following afternoon. That night I left Syria. I had to."

There it was. The mystery was solved. Everyone understood Mr. Bridge did what many Syrians had to do to survive.

"One thing I must ask you," said Mr. Bridge.

"The players, on all teams, are a combination of Shia and Sunni. Our committee made that mandatory. Victor, are you okay with that?"

Victor nodded. "Shia and Sunni and Christian players were on my own team at school."

Mr. Bridge looked at Mom and Dad. They made a joint decision to ask for the agreement, read it and sign.

"Victor, you are the last player to be signed," Mr. Bridge said, sipping his coffee. "Our team is registered as the GTA Gazelles, representing the Greater Toronto Area."

Victor looked at Dad and they both smiled. Gazelles had been Grampa's favourite animals.

The trial was over. The defendants were acquitted. The judges were satisfied. The jury was dismissed. Justice had been served — with coffee and sweet *baklawa* pastries.

Victor went to sleep overjoyed. But he was nervous at the prospect of playing with a new team. His fourth team in just a few months.

His first team was Victor United, with his Syrian friends at school. They had combined with Ozzie's team, Ozzie United, to form Hall United and play the Kingston Bluffers. Then there was the Scarborough Tigers. What would it be like to go back to playing with only other Syrian boys? And how would they do against other teams of Syrians?

4
New Captain

Victor arrived early at Sheppard Soccer Complex. It was the home to several teams, including the season-retired Scarborough Tigers. He found Coach Bridge's office. His new coach welcomed him.

"One more thing before you head out, Victor," said Mr. Bridge. "I saw your friendly match last November against the division champs, the Kingston Bluffers."

"You were there?"

"I've been scouting players since last fall. It was an unforgettable match."

"We had fun," Victor grinned sheepishly.

Who says you cannot go home again? Victor thought as he walked onto the green turf. He never imagined he would be here again, exactly one week after walking out on his team. Victor felt renewed. This turf held good memories. He waved to Dad and Gabriel in the bleachers.

"Goalkeepers must not be on time — they must be early," he recalled Ozzie saying. He missed Ozzie being on the same team.

New Captain

Players and parents began to arrive. When everyone was there Coach Bridge stood in the middle of a circle of thirteen players. He was holding a shiny new red and green soccer ball. He made a slow revolution, looking at each face and smiling, and then he stopped.

"Please don't start crying," Victor whispered to himself.

"*As-salam alaikum*," Coach Bridge said, wishing God's peace upon the team.

"*Wa-laikum as-salam*," they all responded, returning the greeting.

"Welcome. I have met you all one at a time, along with your parents and guardians. I thank you for agreeing to be a part of this tournament. Together you are the GTA Gazelles. From now on, only English will be spoken on and off the field."

As Coach Bridge pointed to each player, including the two subs, they each said their first name and position. The players started looking around. Victor wondered who was going to captain the team. Victor was last. All eyes were on him, and he could hear the whispers.

Mr. Bridge pointed at Victor and said, "And your team captain."

"Victor, goalkeeper," Victor said in a strong voice, despite his surprise.

For their first practice, the team of Syrian refugees did standard drills and activities. The players had been part of indoor leagues across the GTA, and most had played against each other at some point.

During the break Victor overheard one player say, "I have more league experience than Victor. I should be captain, Johnny. And I would never quit on my team." Victor recognized the player as a defender and the back-up goalkeeper.

"Right, Raja. We didn't even get to vote," said Johnny, another defender.

Victor filed away the comments in his head.

For the last activity of the day, everyone lined up to take penalty shots on goal from the twelve-yard penalty spot. Each player would have three turns.

As defender, Raja would rarely be in a position to score on goal. But for every turn he kicked the ball hard — straight at Victor. Each time Victor felt his gloves vibrate as he stopped the ball.

Some balls did get past Victor into the net. But by jumping high, diving, punching balls with fisted gloves and recovering quickly he passed the test. He was their goalkeeper and captain.

Afterwards everyone, including parents, met in Party Room B for pizza and juice.

"Good first day, Victor," Coach Bridge said.

"Yeah —" Victor was unsure of what else to say.

"It went better than I expected."

"You chose the team well, Coach. There's some talent here."

"Any concerns about anyone?"

"None, Coach."

New Captain

"Okay," Coach Bridge said, patting Victor on the shoulder.

As Victor turned away, Johnny ran into him and spilled juice on his boot.

"Sorry, Victor," he said.

"It's — fine," Victor said.

"I didn't mean to. I'll get a paper towel."

"You don't have to. Johnny, right?"

"Yep."

Victor had to believe that the spill was a real mistake, even though he knew Johnny had agreed with Raja that Victor shouldn't be captain. He excused himself, went to the table, tore some paper towels from a roll and cleaned his boot.

The practice schedule was set for Saturdays, Sundays, Tuesdays and Thursdays. Coach Bridge told them that having only a few weeks to prepare would be okay. They had all been playing during the winter and were in good shape. Practices would include more drills, and there would be activities for the players to get to know each other better.

That evening Victor got a call from Ozzie.

"Well, Victor, anything to report?" Ozzie chuckled.

"All quiet," he replied. He told Ozzie about being named captain. He related Raja's overheard comment.

"Welcome to the big leagues as a leader, friend," said Ozzie. "Even if you had been voted in, there would still be some fool thinking he was better than you."

"Yeah. What's up with you?" Victor wanted to change the subject.

"Enjoying retirement," Ozzie joked. "Feels good not to have any planned activities for a change. I'm catching up on my reading."

"I know how much soccer interfered with your reading this winter," Victor teased.

"They're predicting a snowstorm at the end of the week. How about taking out the toboggans next weekend?"

Victor knew it was going to be a busy weekend. "I'll let you know."

"I will take that as a maybe," Ozzie said. "Have fun tomorrow."

"You, too," Victor said, clicking off.

The third Monday of February was a holiday in the province of Ontario, called Family Day. It marked the first long weekend in the year. It sent the message, *Winter is almost over. Hang in there. You'll make it to the end. Spring is coming!*

On the holiday Monday, Victor woke and performed ablution and salat as usual. Then he slept again until eight, when a sound woke him.

Dad seemed to be in good spirits. He was singing a Syrian love song in harmony with Mom. Yep, Syria's

Got Talent was live in the Bayazid residence. The voting starts — now.

Victor smiled to himself. After two and a half years in Canada, Dad was still working as an accounting assistant, even though he had been an experienced accountant in Syria. Mom volunteered at a local daycare, and also worked three mornings a week as a dental hygienist to help out with the finances. Victor was aware of Dad's frustration with not being the sole financial provider of the family. So it was good to hear Dad being happy.

There was no snow in the overcast sky when Dad parked the family Toyota. He led them into the vast Scarborough Town Centre and toward the new food court. Dad treated them to a lunch of lentil soup, falafels and juice. The regular stores were closed, leaving them to window shop, lost in silent desires and wishes.

Dad had been given a family movie pass to the Cineplex. Mom chose a comedy she had heard about. As the previews ran, Mom shared baggies of almonds, dried apricots and figs.

The movie started. Even though Victor laughed along with his family and a theatre filled with strangers, his mind kept flashing on Grampa. The fourth anniversary of his death was one week away. Mom and Dad had not spoken about it, but he knew it must also be on their minds.

Will it come and go quickly? he wondered.

5
Setting the Past Straight

Victor was the first student out the school doors when the buzzer sounded. His first bus was Neilson. At Sheppard, he transferred to his second bus. The extra-long TTC bus took him east, past Morningside, to Sheppard Soccer Complex.

At the main door, he saw Coach Jeong-Hough entering with two empty cardboard boxes. "Hello, Victor," she said.

"Hi, Coach," he replied. It was the first time they had spoken since his release from the team.

"I know that you're rushing to practice," she said.

How did she know? Oh, yes, some adults know everything.

"Walk with me for a minute," she said. "I meant to call you last night." They walked past the weight room and the snack bar. "But I've been busy wrapping up the season and clearing out my office. Actually, this is better, face to face."

Or profile to profile, he thought. *What can she have to say to me?*

"I want to apologize to you, Victor. I should have trusted you. You have always been dependable. I should have listened to you."

"Okay —"

"Yesterday, I was told that Randy Harris from the North York Engineers tripped the goalkeeper during a playoff match on Sunday. It was caught on a parent's phone camera." They entered her near-empty office. "I'm so sorry, Victor. Please forgive me."

"Sure," he said shrugging. "You didn't see it." In his mind, he thought of that month's school character trait that Principal Arsenault had announced. *Truthfulness. Wow, it did work*, he thought, relieved.

"Randy Harris is out of the league. If you want to come back next season, I'll hold a spot for you. Let me know. And I'll send an official apology in writing to your parents."

"Okay, Coach."

"And also let them know that Coach Bridge is a man of his word. He did not try to steal you away from our team. Good luck with the tournament," she said, holding out her hand for Victor to shake. "And, Victor, if you need any help with anything at all, just ask."

By Saturday's practice the news had spread through the soccer community. Everyone knew Victor's goal was not his fault. Everyone knew he had reason to walk out.

"You're still a quitter in my books," Raja said as he passed Victor in the change room.

Once again, Victor ignored him.

The main drill that afternoon involved dribbling and passing. Each player was holding a ball and they were spread out across the whole field.

Coach Bridge blew his whistle to get their attention. "First you will dribble your ball moving around. Aim to cover the field. You must touch the ball two hundred times using all parts of your feet."

He blew his whistle and they started. Some boys started to laugh as they lost control of the ball and lost count.

"Keep going. No touching of the ball with your hands even if it goes out of bounds. Focus," Coach Bridge shouted.

When they were bent over, panting, Coach Bridge blew his whistle again. "Take slow, deep breaths," he advised. "This time after ten touches you will look for a teammate, call his name and pass your ball to him. And he will pass his ball to you. Keep going. Avoid having the balls strike each other. It does not matter who you pass the ball to. Aim to have an exchange with everyone on the field."

In this drill, Victor managed to pass to every player. He even passed to Raja, who seemed to be enjoying himself.

After the break Coach Bridge announced a thirty-five minute straight six-on-seven match. He and Victor had worked out the teams beforehand.

"Time to see how well you've been learning from the drills," Coach Bridge said, as he passed the list to Victor.

"Team One," Victor announced. "Six players. Me in goal and captain. Forwards are Habib and Nabil. Midfielders are Dani and Malik. Bassel on defence."

The players he called moved behind him. He continued, "Team Two. Raja as goalkeeper and captain. Forwards are Muta and Anwar. Midfielders, Malik, Firas and Hayyan. Johnny on defence."

Victor had decided to put one of the subs, Bassel and Joram, on each team to avoid complaints from Raja. Victor gave himself fewer players. No one could accuse him of taking advantage.

Each team huddled to discuss strategy. Two minutes later Raja won the coin toss. Coach Bridge, as ref, blew the whistle. Muta kicked off to Anwar. And they were off.

At the scoreless halfway mark, Coach Bridge called out, "Two minute break."

All the players grabbed bottles of water. The teams sat huddled together.

"Guys, you're playing well defensively," Victor started. "Time to take it to them."

"But we're outnumbered," Habib protested.

"That's all right. Just play full out. See what

happens. This is an exercise. You're not playing for a cup," Victor said.

Then he recalled playing six-on-seven with his team, Victor United. *I was their captain. I have been a leader before. This new captain's role is a chance to do it again. Only this time the stakes are much higher.*

Victor's strategy worked at first. Joram scored quickly, assisted by Habib. Then Raja's team came back like a boomerang. Forward Muta scored on Victor, and then midfielder Malik did. In the end, Raja's team celebrated a 2–1 victory. Victor was not disappointed. Raja was the one who needed the boost in confidence.

"That's how you captain a team," Raja said so only Victor could hear.

There was no time for Victor to respond. Coach Bridge brought the entire team in a wide circle, where they sat exhausted.

"Congratulations, Team Raja. This exercise was not to see who would win. It was to see how well you play together, especially having fewer teammates on each line. You all did well. Passed the ball. Dribbled with control."

"We had a lot of field to cover," midfielder Dani spoke up.

"Yes, but you all played full out. That was good. It conditions you. Well done, players."

He dismissed them and gave Victor a thumbs-up sign.

The next day Coach Bridge called another six-on-seven match. This time they played two thirty-five minute halves, so they'd be playing twice as long. He switched team captains so that Victor could work with the other players. Victor could see how he was shaping up as a solo captain.

A storm had brought lots of soft snow. Victor planned to meet Ozzie after practice at Neilson Park, and Gabriel had begged to come along. Victor was not sure. Gabriel was just over another cold. In the end, Victor decided to take his brother with him.

Victor, Gabriel and Ozzie enjoyed tobogganing down a mound of snow. They bounced and flew through the air on magical plastic carpets the same size as Victor's prayer rug. Victor didn't often get to have that kind of fun outdoors. What pleased him most was seeing the expression of pure joy on Gabriel's face.

"He's like a child, Ozzie," said Victor.

"He *is* a child, Victor. What, you think you're grown up all of a sudden?"

"We are growing up. I've been feeling it. Soon we'll graduate and be in high school."

"I hear you," Ozzie said. He packed some snow into his glove to form a snowball. "You know what? We're not there yet." And he pitched the snowball square onto Victor's forehead.

The snowball fight that followed proved Ozzie's words.

Victor made hot chocolate when he and Gabriel got home. Their parents were out visiting friends in the building. Gabriel read some of Victor's older comic books in their bedroom. Victor caught a glimpse of the setting sun from their tenth-floor living-room window. He picked up a sketch he had been working on to add another image. The only sound in the room was his charcoal pencil scratching the rough surface of the 9-inch by 12-inch paper. It began to blend in with another sound that seemed to come from far away.

A beat-up soccer ball rolls along a dusty patch of earth. Victor, Mom, Dad, Gabriel and Grampa walk along a highway. Thousands have fled their homes all over the country to save their lives. Loved ones and neighbours have disappeared or been killed, including lots of children. Cities continue to be bombed and taken over by troops. The Bayazid family pauses along the highway to rest and eat a few mouthfuls of food. Grampa is repeating his mantra that family is the most important thing. Gabriel kicks the ball to Victor. Without trapping it to control it, Victor kicks it and it rolls onto the highway —

The sound of Mom and Dad coming in the door brought Victor back to the present. He hid the sketch, putting it away to finish after supper.

6
Reaching Out

The next morning Victor presented the completed sketch to Mom and Dad at breakfast. It was the third anniversary of Grampa's death. The picture showed the sun setting behind a mountain range. In the front, stood Grampa. His face showed a mixture of fear and confusion. He was holding a beat-up, dusty soccer ball.

"I'll buy a frame for it, Victor," Mom said, breaking the silence. She was near tears.

"Son, let the past be the past," Dad said flatly.

Victor found that hard to do. He knew that Dad blamed him for Grampa's death.

"Victor, your drawings are really good," Gabriel beamed. "You should make a graphic book."

When Gabriel started to cough, Victor thought nothing of it.

At Tuesday's practice Victor arrived early, as usual. He and some of the other Gazelles jogged around the field and began stretching to warm up. The others would begin on time by four-thirty. Coach Bridge was not strict about the weekdays because he knew that snow, icy roads and slower traffic could cause delays. Also, only Victor, midfielder Dani and sub Bassel lived in Scarborough. The others came from across the other parts of the GTA.

In nine days they would leave for Vancouver. But Victor still did not feel like they were a solid team. In the first half of practice they worked in separate groups: forwards, midfielders defenders. The subs helped Victor with goalkeeper exercises. But they all seemed to be just going through the motions. There was no spark, no fire.

"Maybe they're tired," Victor said to Coach Bridge at the break. "We all have school assignments due before March Break."

"You might have a point there," Coach Bridge said. "The weekend was quite intense."

"I have an idea," Victor offered.

"I'm listening."

"The team could be ready for a real match."

"Who would we play against?" Coach Bridge asked.

"Toronto FC," Victor said. Then he chuckled. "I'm kidding, Coach. An Under-14 team. If I can arrange it, would you agree to next Saturday afternoon?"

"Yes. It might be the focus everyone needs."

"I'll let you know what I find out by tomorrow."

They agreed not to say anything to the team until it was confirmed.

When Victor got home Dad waved an envelope in the air.

"That Coach Jeong-Huffy . . ."

"Hough," Victor corrected Dad.

"Hough," Dad pronounced correctly. "She has honour. She put her apology in writing. I'm impressed." He showed Victor the letter.

It was excellent timing. Victor phoned Coach Jeong-Hough. After all, she had offered to help him.

"It's short notice, Victor," Coach Jeong-Hough said once Victor had outlined his plan. "I'll get back to you in a while."

In the meantime Victor phoned the one person who would need no convincing — Ozzie. About an hour later Coach Jeong-Hough got back to Victor. "You're lucky. I have most of the Tigers on board. The others will let me know tomorrow. If they're not free, I'll get a couple of the Kingston Bluffers at school. Either way, it's happening."

"Thanks, Coach."

"For you and Mr. Bridge? Anytime."

Victor phoned Coach Bridge with the news.

"That was fast, Victor. Good job," he said. "I'll let

everyone know. And I've decided to cancel Thursday's practice. We'll have the first part of Saturday's training session to practice strategies."

Victor went to sleep that night with a smile on his face. It was all coming together. He was taking care of important duties as captain.

By Wednesday morning Gabriel had a head cold. Victor was worried. He thought about how wet and cold they got in the snow. He remembered how tired Gabriel was when they got home. Did he make a mistake taking Gabriel out on the weekend?

At school Principal Arsenault announced the character word for March: *Forgiveness*.

Victor felt that Coach Bridge giving them Thursday as a practice-free day was good for the team. But he wanted to keep working on his skills. How would he feel if the team lost because he wasn't prepared? How would the team feel?

Victor talked with Mr. Greenidge, his coach from the match they had played in the fall. He agreed to let Victor use the school gym for twenty minutes before school on Thursday and Friday morning. Victor got Muhammad to take shots at him. Ozzie gave him goalkeeping pointers and corrected his movements and timing.

By Saturday morning, Gabriel was feeling no better. Mom decided to take him to the health clinic at Malvern Town Centre. Gabriel was disappointed. He had been hoping to go with Dad to watch Victor play.

"The cold is in his chest now," Mom said. "I don't want it to get worse."

Victor thought about forgiveness. Dad had not forgiven Victor for what happened to Grampa. Would Mom forgive him if he confessed he had let Gabriel get sick?

Victor sat in Coach Bridge's office to go over the schedule. They had the field from noon to three o'clock. The first forty-five minutes they would work on team strategy. Then a fifteen-minute break. The Tigers would arrive by one o'clock to change and begin their warm-up. Kickoff at one-thirty. Coach Jeong-Hough had paid for a league referee and two lines-people.

They would play two thirty-five-minute halves with a ten-minute break. Coach Bridge explained that this would be the time scheduled for each game at the tournament. Most Under-14 matches had two forty-five-minute halves. But since the players would be playing matches for a week, the shorter format would be easier on everyone.

The Gazelles warmed up and started their session.

"Guys, this is only going to be a rehearsal match," Coach Bridge started. "I want you to take some risks. Make mistakes here instead of at the tournament. Find out where you need to improve. Be aware of where your teammates are on the field. Know what you need to do in your position."

Coach Bridge created strategies for the forwards Habib and Muta. Next were the midfielders: Dani, Hayyan, Firas and Malik. He worked out how forwards and midfielders would work together. Finally, he worked with defenders Raja, Johnny, Nabil and Anwar. The defenders, rather than playing across the field in a line, would be in a diamond formation. Johnny would be slightly ahead at the top point of the diamond in the role of *sweeper*. It would be his duty to sweep the ball away from the defence area. Nabil and Anwar would be just behind at the right and left sides of the field. The line at the bottom point of the diamond was the *stopper* — the fiercest and most dangerous of the defenders, Raja. The subs, Joram and Bassel, would play in the second half.

If the ball got past the diamond of defenders, Victor was the only one left to fully protect the goal. The key was how well the defenders and the goalkeeper worked together. Would Raja follow Victor's instructions?

7
Rehearsal Match

The Gazelles took their break. Coach Jeong-Hough and some early-bird Tigers arrived and began to warm up. But things do not always go as planned, in life and in soccer.

At 1:25 p.m. Coach Jeong-Hough approached Coach Bridge and Victor. "I'm still two players short. Everyone was confirmed. I've tried calling their parents, with no luck," she said.

Coach Bridge looked at his watch. "We have to be off the field by three o'clock. Two other teams are already booked."

When Victor walked out of the Tigers game, the two missing players had been among his loudest critics. He felt in his gut that they were not going to see those two players.

"I have an idea," Victor said. "Our subs, Joram and Bassel, were going to be playing the second half. Instead, we will put them on the Tigers. One midfielder and one defender."

"No subs for either team. I can live with that," Coach Bridge said.

"Deal." Coach Jeong-Hough beamed. "Victor, you're shaping up to be quite the leader."

I still have to prove that, Victor thought.

Kickoff was at 1:40 p.m. The first half was very energetic. Both teams displayed their skills, especially the forwards when they had the ball. Habib scored first against Ozzie in the Tigers goal at the twenty-eight-minute mark. Victor and the Gazelles managed to hold the lead till halftime.

They started late, so break was cut to eight minutes. The Gazelles huddled, sipping water and eating oranges.

"Guys, you're working well as a team. I like what I'm seeing. Remember everything we practised and talked about before," Coach Bridge said. "Anything you want to share, Victor?"

Victor did not hesitate. "I know this team a bit," he began, to chuckles. "They are a strong comeback team. Coach Jeong-Hough would have told them at the start to play fast and hard, to treat us as a seasoned team. And you saw that. But don't think they don't have anything in reserve. So, guys, this is no Saturday afternoon —" Victor searched for the phrase, "—'let's kick the ball around' match. They are going to come back at us with all they've got. One last thing. Forwards and defenders, don't expect Joram and Bassel to be easy on you."

True to Victor's prediction, the Tigers stormed

back with a vengeance in the second half. They held possession of the ball most of the time. The Gazelles struggled to keep pace with a team that played as if it was a regional final.

Victor saved many shots on goal. He barely had a moment to relax. He punted the ball into the Tigers half of the field, but their forwards and midfielders brought it back toward him in what seemed to be seconds.

The defence, especially Raja, was working hard. In three minutes the match would be over. Victory shone on the horizon like a newly risen sun. Victor could hardly wait.

Sometimes victory can be blinding.

"Raja, watch out for that guy on your left!" Victor yelled to the defender.

But it was too late.

The charging Tigers striker, Muhammad, faked a move that sent Raja in the wrong direction to his right side. Victor stepped to his left side to cover his corner. In that split second he left the middle of the goal free and clear for the Tigers midfielder and captain, Raymond, to tap the ball across the goal line. The score was tied at 1–1.

Victor was angry with himself. He knew he should admire the skilful play. But it stung to be beaten by a former teammate.

"Recover, Victor, recover," he whispered to himself.

He bowled the ball back to the ref while the Tigers

celebrated. Victor's not-at-this-moment-buddy, Ozzie, was in the thick of it. But Victor knew they would be buddies again in two minutes.

Victor had played a lot of games and watched a lot of matches on TV. He knew that the final two minutes of any match were sometimes the most dangerous.

There was what might be called the final kickoff. All were tired. The Gazelles forwards passed the ball between each other. Flanked by two of their midfielders, Dani and Firas, they bolted toward the Tigers defence, only to lose possession of the ball. Tigers defender Drew sent the ball back to Ozzie. And he punted the ball back into the Gazelles territory. It was a punt-for-punt move, as if he was saying to Victor, "You punt, I punt."

Victor was determined not to be scored on at the end of the match. All of the Tigers advanced in a wave.

Ten seconds left.

Ozzie had left the goal empty. The Tigers kept coming.

Five seconds left.

Victor had trouble seeing the ball as his defenders braced for the attack.

Two seconds.

Whistle!

It was all over. Victor knew how lucky he was. *Another five seconds, and who knows*, he thought.

In Party Room A, they all gathered for a pizza party. As Raja passed by Victor he whispered, "You'll have to do a lot better if we're gonna win any matches in Vancouver."

Victor stared at him. *Is he going to be a problem?* Victor wondered.

Victor approached Coach Bridge just as he was saying to Coach Jeong-Hough, "Thanks for the workout."

"You didn't expect us to go easy on you, did you?" she asked.

"I was hoping your team wouldn't squash us. That might have rattled their confidence heading into the tournament. As it is, I'm pleased with the outcome." Coach Bridge smiled.

Victor was not pleased. He was relieved. He had his concerns about the overall strength of the team. He also worried about them trusting him as a captain. So sometimes — sometimes — relief was okay.

8
The Push to Get Better

Early Sunday morning, Victor had gone through ablution and salat with every muscle aching and sleep grogginess filling his head. Gabriel's wheezing from his chest cold had woken Victor several times through the night.

When Victor woke up for the second time at eight o'clock on Sunday morning he felt better rested. But Gabriel still sounded bad.

Is he getting better or worse? Victor wondered.

"Victor, honey," said Mom. "I'm going to get in touch with my old friend, Amira Wassef. I heard she ended up in Vancouver after her husband and two of hers sons died."

"How did they die?" Victor asked.

"They were on one of the boats heading to Greece when it turned over and everyone drowned. She and her other son, Abbas, were not with them."

"That's sad."

"Yes, we heard many stories like that. That's why we went to Lebanon," Mom said. "You remember

Abbas, don't you? You played together one weekend when we went to Aleppo."

"No."

"Five years ago?"

Victor shook his head.

"Anyhow, you'll see him again."

Victor shrugged. He had no memory of this Abbas.

The Gazelles sat on the field in a circle. Coach Bridge stood holding a soccer ball. For a split second Victor saw Grampa standing, holding the ball in the same way. He blinked and the image was gone.

"I am happy that you finally got to work as a team yesterday. And that brings me to another point. Communication," Coach Bridge said. "Forwards, midfielders, are you guys on the same team? We'll work on that today. I want each of you communicating silently and vocally with your line as well as with every other teammate, including your goalkeeper."

"Yes, Coach," they said together.

"Another issue," he continued. He put down the ball and picked up his clipboard to consult his notes. "Passing. Dani and Firas, you two more than anyone else are guilty of wild passes of a moving ball. I want you to practise stopping the ball before an opponent is close to you. Take your time. Then pass. You'll have more control. A spinning ball is harder to control."

Victor thought that Coach Bridge was being fair and thorough. And he finally saw why he was giving notes now, rather than after the practice match. Coach Bridge did not want to spoil the good feelings the team had from completing their first full match. Victor slotted away the idea. He wanted to be a strong leader and help his team get better, too.

"You all ran out of steam in the last ten minutes," Coach Bridge went on. "That must not happen again. The more you control the ball, the more you control the pace of the match. Understood?"

"Yes, Coach."

The team worked on all these things during the first half of the practice. After the break, they sat in a circle once more.

A week earlier they had been given a tournament package with information to take home. But Coach Bridge explained that if they heard some things aloud, the information could stick in their memory.

"You are guaranteed a match against each of the other teams," Coach Bridge started. "Four eastern teams. Four western teams. By the end of Round #7, the eastern team with the most points will play the western team with the most points in a final." He paused to make sure they understood, then continued. "There's no extra time for stoppage added on. If there's a draw after seventy minutes, that's it. No penalty shootouts, except in the final, if necessary."

They went on to practise more drills. Coach Bridge worked individually with Victor to sharpen his skills.

When he ended the practice, Coach Bridge reminded them to get lots of rest. Victor did not need to hear that twice. He was willing to stuff his ears with cotton balls to get a better sleep that night.

Victor finished the last of his school assignments that evening. And he stuffed his ears with cotton balls, just in case Gabriel did have another restless night. Victor knew Gabriel was spitting up yellow mucus. He wished it was clear. Or, better still, no mucus at all. If Gabriel showed some sign of getting better, Victor would feel happy. He'd feel happy for his brother. And he would feel better about taking him tobogganing the weekend before. These were Victor's last thoughts as the sleep guardian escorted him through the night clouds high in the sky.

On Monday morning Gabriel's mucus was dark. His lips had a blue tint. His chest was aching when he took a breath. He wouldn't eat. Mom confirmed that his fever was high. She and Dad prepared to take him to the emergency department at Scarborough Centenary hospital, just south of the Malvern area. Victor left for school worried, aware that Gabriel was sicker.

Mom texted Victor that Gabriel had pneumonia and the hospital was keeping him for a couple of days. After school Ozzie went with Victor to the hospital. When they arrived Gabriel was sleeping with tubes in his nostrils to ease his breathing.

After visiting hours were over, Victor, Mom and Ozzie waited for Dad to get the car and drive them home. Dad would return to stay overnight with Gabriel.

"I'm going to call Coach Bridge and tell him I won't go to Vancouver," Victor suddenly stated.

"Are you crazy?" Ozzie exclaimed.

"Victor, what makes you say that? Did something happen on the team?" Mom asked.

"If I don't go I'll be able to stay with Gabriel. It's my fault. I took him tobogganing. He's so sick," Victor sobbed.

Mom put her arm around him and he buried his head in her shoulder.

"Honey, you did nothing wrong," said Mom. "Gabriel could have caught pneumonia anywhere. Even from school."

"Your mom's right. Don't blame yourself," Ozzie added. "Look, your ticket's already bought. You're the captain. Who would replace you?"

Victor dried his eyes with his scarf. He thought of Raja replacing him as captain and goalkeeper. Raja would get his wish. *No way,* Victor thought. Not after how hard he had worked.

"Victor, Gabriel is in good hands here," said Mom. "Think about why this tournament is being held. You are representing Syrians from all over the country to say thanks to Canada. That includes people who can't be there, like the rest of our family."

Victor nodded. He would represent Gabriel and say thank you to the country offering Gabriel medical care. "I'll go. I must go," he said.

But Victor could still feel the guilt hanging over him like a dark rain cloud. It was a lot like the guilt he felt about Grampa.

Sleep did not come easily to Victor. When it did, he surrendered to it like a stone dropped in a pond.

9
Last Chance

Moments before the start of practice on Tuesday, Coach Bridge phoned Victor. He told him that he was running late and to get the team started.

Victor got off the phone and took a deep breath. He was not sure how his teammates would react. His head was swirling. But he knew that he had to act responsibly. That gave him a sudden rush of energy.

Victor gathered the Gazelles and explained the situation. There were rumblings. Some wanted to wait for Coach Bridge. Victor reminded them that it was their last practice. They could not afford to waste any time. He led them through a warm-up. Then he opened his notebook for two seconds and closed it.

"This drill is called Split Defence."

He tossed a ball to forwards Habib and Muta, and another one to Bassel and Joram.

"All right, two midfielders will join each pair of forwards."

Midfielders Dani and Hayyan went with Habib and

Muta, while midfielders Firas and Malik sided with Bassel and Joram.

"Both groups will attack at the same time. The four defenders — Raja, Nabil, Anwar and Johnny — will decide among themselves how to defend the goal," Victor concluded, looking around.

"How about if we stand aside and see how you handle two balls at once," Johnny joked. Some of the players chuckled.

"This is silly. There will never be two balls on the field at the same time in a real game," Raja sneered.

"Guys, this is an exercise," Victor said with authority. He looked squarely at Raja before continuing. "If you don't want to do it, you can get off the field now."

No one moved.

"Take your positions, please!" he barked.

By the fourth time the forwards and midfielders attacked the goal, the defence had worked out strategies. They were also communicating better among themselves.

When Victor had opened and closed his notebook before, it was on a blank page. He had made up the activity on the spot. He would write it down later from memory.

So far, he had made the right decisions as captain. *Will I continue to do so?* he wondered.

Then Coach Bridge arrived and he thanked Victor for leading the team. Victor had seen him crouching near the doorway from the second run of the activity.

Coach Bridge led them through the rest of the practice. And then he answered last-minute questions about the tournament.

"It's March Break. Who will watch us play?" Dani asked.

"Allah will watch you play," Johnny responded.

That got laughs from them all, including Coach Bridge.

"The spectators will be children from various schools, anyone who has an interest in soccer. All tickets are free. But instead of teachers, they will be there with parents and guardians," Coach Bridge replied.

"Syrians?"

"Syrians, yes, and other children. Any more questions?"

Raja raised his hand. "The package said bunk beds. Four to a room. Do we have a choice of roommates?"

Raja locked eyes with Victor who held his gaze. Victor already knew the answer and smiled inwardly.

"The short answer is no," explained Coach Bridge. "All teams are made up of eleven players plus two subs. The four defenders will room together. The four midfielders will room together. Goalkeeper, two forwards and two subs will room together with an extra cot. You will decide among yourselves who gets which spot when you see the rooms."

While the players thought about the room assignments, Coach Bridge reminded them, "You are doing something unique and special. I believe your captain has one last thing to share with you."

Victor stood in the middle of the circle. "Since we are the GTA Gazelles, this will be our motto: G for Great, T for Team and A for Attitude."

Victor stuck out his hand. In twos and threes the rest of the team came to the centre, placing their hands on top of one another's. Raja's was the last hand in.

"Great, Team, Attitude!" they shouted in unison.

Victor hoped he was sending a message.

And then they were dismissed.

⚽ ⚽ ⚽

Victor knew that Principal Arsenault was kind and fair-minded. And he believed she liked him. So he was curious when she called Victor into her office for a meeting. Principals from schools across the GTA were aware of the Syrian project. They all had given permission for March Break to start early for the players in the tournament.

They chatted casually for a few minutes.

"I know that you are representing your cultural heritage, Victor. And I am proud of you for what you are doing," she said. "I also want to remind you that you are representing William Hall PS."

"Yes, Principal Arsenault. Thanks," Victor responded.

They stood and shook hands.

The unspoken message was clear: we expect great things from you, Victor mused.

"I hope you get to Stanley Park. It's quite special," she added.

Victor nodded and managed a shy smile.

On Wednesday after school, Victor went back to the hospital. This time he was alone. He did not get close to Gabriel. He feared passing on any germs from the outside to make his condition worse. So, he sent him a silent message to get well quickly. "Allah is healing you. I'll see you soon, my brother," he whispered.

Seeing Gabriel so sick brought tears to Victor's eyes.

Mom had packed Victor's suitcase by the time he arrived home.

"Here is Abbas's phone number," she said, handing him a slip of paper. "His mom says he's excited to see you again. Especially since he's on the Vancouver Herons team."

"Okay. That means I get to play against him. I wonder what position he plays."

As Victor picked up his suitcase, he saw something new on the sideboard in the living room. It was the sketch of Grampa. Mom had set it in a silver frame, as she promised.

It was the last thing Victor looked at before leaving home.

10
Where Soccer Takes You

The last time Victor was at Pearson International Airport, his family was arriving in Canada. That was at nighttime. Victor looked around at the morning travellers in the brightly lit terminal. He felt somewhat alone even though he was with a different family, a sports family. He now understood Coach Bridge's decision to travel a day early. He recalled last year's TV news coverage of March Break. The stories of thousands of people at airports and flight delays. March Break Madness, they had called it. They were able to avoid that.

Outside snow was falling, but it was not storming. Victor hoped he had seen the last of that winter.

They boarded the WestJet plane with no fuss. No one was left behind. Nothing had to be taken away by security. Everyone followed airport rules.

And then the plane took off. Clouds, clouds and more clouds! That was all Victor saw from his window seat. Dani snored beside him while the others bobbed their heads listening to music or watched an in-flight movie.

Victor worked on a drawing in a new sketchbook Mom had packed in his carry-on bag. In it, Coach Bridge's eyes were looking up as if seeing the soccer ball balanced on top of his groomed hair. But Victor's thoughts were not really on the sketch. They were on the things Islam stood for, including peace, tolerance and forgiveness. His mind focused on Randy Harris and the way he had kicked Victor to make that goal. If that goal had not been allowed the Tigers might have made the playoffs and —

Victor had been angry at Randy Harris over the past few weeks. Now he silently forgave him. It surprised him that he felt no anger at Randy.

Wow! That felt easy, Victor thought, *easier than when I had that fight with Ozzie last September and we had to apologize to each other in front of Principal Arsenault.* Because of Randy Harris's wrongdoing, Victor was on a plane to play soccer for a whole week, against Syrian players from all parts of Canada.

Later, the plane descended and the snowy Rocky Mountains came into view. The ragged peaks reminded Victor of Syria. Lower, still, the city began to take shape. Sunlight flooded skyscrapers, homes, vehicles moving like insects, greenery and the ocean. The plane finally bounced onto land at Vancouver International Airport.

The Gazelles collected their luggage. Just outside the luggage claim hall, they were greeted by the local organizers of the Syrian Soccer Youth Thank You Canada Tournament.

The Gazelles were taken to the grounds of University of British Columbia, or UBC. They arrived at the newly renovated National Soccer Development Centre, called NSDC.

"If you want to make soccer your career, NSDC is the sports temple, sports mosque, sports church, sports Mecca," said one of the organizers, Mr. Sanders, chuckling. "Home of the Vancouver Whitecaps FC development program."

I'm not thinking that far ahead in my career, thought Victor. *But it's good to know.*

The air was fresh with a cool breeze. Victor found the contrast with the freezing winds back home magical. One moment he was in winter, the next he was in spring. He thought about when Ozzie said, "Spring is coming," as a joke. It was Victor's reality sooner than he had thought.

Once inside the NSDC, the Gazelles were met by the three volunteer assistants for their team. Amena, Sandra and Lilith were Syrian students at UBC. Some of the players acted silly. Victor guessed that was what happened when boys met pretty older girls.

The Gazelles settled into their dorm rooms. Victor chose a top bunk, just like at home. He would be able to sketch there without anyone noticing.

When they toured the Centre, Victor remembered

that the first seven rounds of matches would take place at the same time on four of the Centre's five fields. Three were grass and two were turf. Victor spotted two other teams being escorted around. He wondered if Abbas was on one of them, or if he got to come to the Centre all the time.

Each player was given a "burner" cell phone with limited minutes to call home. Victor called Mom and Dad right away. They told him there was no change to Gabriel's condition.

"Focus on your trip, honey," Mom said. "We'll all be fine here."

Victor phoned Abbas. It turned out Abbas was at the Centre with his team, the Vancouver Herons. Victor and Abbas agreed to meet before dinner in the hallway outside the prayer rooms set aside for Shias and Sunnis to pray separately. The rooms were to be used for salat and for personal silence. Victor chose the location because he still couldn't remember ever meeting Abbas.

After a rest in their rooms, on which Coach Bridge insisted and the players took without argument, Victor went to meet Abbas. To his surprise, he recognized Abbas right away. Both were now thirteen and the same height. They talked about the weekend their families had spent together, a long time ago when they were small children. They now looked at each other as almost-grown-up teenagers.

"I see that we play each other on Saturday," Abbas said.

"Yep. On grass."

"That your favourite surface?"

"I've been getting used to turf more and more over the winter. Haven't played on grass since November. I hope it doesn't rain," Victor said.

"Yeah, right! You're in Rain-couver, man," Abbas laughed.

"So, are you any good?"

"Just watch me," Abbas replied boldly.

"I guess I'll have to," Victor said smiling.

They walked together to the huge dining hall. It was decorated with soccer posters and photos of Canadian players and teams.

The players collected their food and the teams sat together. A local Imam welcomed them all with a prayer and said the blessing over the food. Victor found the food tasty and looked forward to the meals they would have over the next days. When they had finished there was an announcement that the final match would be at BC Place Stadium, home of the Vancouver Whitecaps FC. Excited chatter filled the dining hall. For a fleeting moment Victor had the fantasy that the Gazelles could be lucky enough to play that final match.

"Slow down, Victor. Seven matches. One at a time," he whispered to himself.

"I encourage all of you to mix and mingle as much as you can. At each meal, sit with a different team. On the field you are friendly competitors. Off the field you are all brothers," Mr. Sanders said in a speech to all the players.

Mix and mingle they did. But Victor was glad to go to bed early. He thought about meeting Abbas, someone he once knew. He tried to recall some of the names of the other players he met. One of the names he found easy to remember was that of a smiling new "brother" called Gabriel.

11
Winning and Losing

Victor entered the prayer room on Friday morning as Raja was leaving. They nodded politely to each other. Later, they made their way to the field.

Teams practised on the same field where they would later have their match. The Gazelles would get Field #1 for their practice first. Victor looked at the day's game schedule posted:

Round #1
1:30–3:00
GTA Gazelles vs. Calgary Oranges

Victor led the morning warm-up. The Gazelles seemed rested and energized. Coach Bridge's main concern for the practice, once again, was communication between the players.

When their field time was up he directed the team inside the Centre to an empty meeting room. While they drank water and juice to rehydrate, Coach Bridge informed them of the game plan. The starters would be the same as in the practice match against the Tigers. The defenders formation, in the shape of a diamond, would have Raja as stopper. He would be closer to Victor in goal. At the head of the diamond Johnny would be sweeper.

"These could be stressful positions. I'll have you alternate during a match or match by match," Coach Bridge said to Raja and Johnny. Both nodded.

"Subs Bassel and Joram, you will play second halves. Bassel, you will switch with defenders Nabil and Anwar. While you, Joram, will switch with either a forward or a midfielder."

Both Bassel and Joram shrugged and smiled. They would be much more than benchwarmers.

"Of course, this is soccer. Anything can happen," Coach Bridge continued. "I don't want any player too tired. You will be playing seven matches."

"I thought you said we would be playing eight, if you include the final," Johnny quipped.

"You do your part, Johnny, and we might be lucky enough to have that happen," Coach Bridge responded. "Soccer does offer lucky chances. But they are backed by solid teamwork."

"What's the intelligence on these Oranges?" Dani asked seriously.

"Some are sour, some are sweet," Johnny said, to many chortles. Even Coach Bridge allowed himself a smile.

"The Department of Agriculture had nothing in

their files to report," Habib joined in.

Victor realized that his teammates were nervous. "There's no intelligence on any team," said Victor. "No videos to study of their tactics. Only a few rumours."

"I overheard some Calgary Oranges saying that they were strong contenders," Raja offered.

"Are we going to take their word for it?" asked Victor.

"Okay, team, you have a half-hour before lunch," Coach Bridge said, looking at his watch.

Victor used some of the time to call home. He was told that Gabriel was getting better. That set him up to head into the first match.

The Gazelles in their bright red shirts won the coin toss and kicked off against the Calgary Oranges. The Oranges midfielders soon wrangled the ball and charged toward the Gazelles defence. The defenders held them off repeatedly. Habib and Muta appeared weak and sluggish to Victor. He wanted his forwards to stop losing the ball so easily. The first half ended scoreless, 0–0. The Oranges had clearly been the aggressors for the first part of the match.

"Forwards, midfielders, wake up!" Coach Bridge yelled. "The defenders can't do all the work here."

The players looked down at their cleats.

"Raise your heads. I don't want you to feel bad. Feeling bad helps no one. I want you to be energized.

It takes goals to win a match. Ask yourselves, 'Am I playing my best?' Get on the field and show me your best in the next thirty-five minutes."

"Great, Team, Attitude!" they shouted in unison.

Early in the second half the Oranges kept hammering at the Gazelles defence. Victor continued to save shots. Then he lunged in the wrong direction. The Oranges took the lead, 0–1.

Did anyone really hear Coach Bridge? Victor wondered. *Did his words bounce off their skulls?*

Only after falling behind in the score did the Gazelles forwards wake up. The passing skills of Habib and Muta got stronger. They communicated with each other and with the midfielders. At the fifty-two-minute mark of the second half Habib scored with a header from a corner kick by midfielder Dani. The score was tied at 1–1. There were eighteen minutes left.

Moments later, midfielder Firas got a breakaway. He sped past a now sluggish Oranges defence and fired one into the upper corner. From then, the Oranges ran out of steam. They had given their all. The Gazelles defence held them off, winning Round #1 with a score of 2–1.

Coach Bridge congratulated the team but said no more. Victor sensed that he wanted to give more detailed notes. They could wait until next morning. Everyone was happy, even Raja.

At dinner, Victor sat at a table with Abbas and players from Montreal and Halifax. Both boys were happy that their teams had won, with Vancouver blanking Montreal 4–0. Abbas had scored his first tournament goal. Victor realized Abbas was a striker he needed to keep an eye on.

Unlike the first match, the Round #2 match was set for Saturday morning to give the teams the afternoon free.

Round #2
9:00–10:30
GTA Gazelles vs. Vancouver Herons

As the match started, Victor quickly saw firsthand what Abbas could do. Victor watched Abbas dance with the ball past the Gazelles midfielders and defenders to face him twice, scoring both times. With eight minutes left in the match Muta answered back for the Gazelles.

Victor watched from his position as his teammates failed to make an equalizer. In the last three minutes, a Herons midfielder shot the ball past Victor. The final score was 1–3 in favour of the Herons.

"You let in three cheap goals, captain," Raja said. But he said it quietly, so only Dani and Victor heard him.

"You could be a better defender, Raja," Dani said, standing up for Victor. "How did those three balls, plus all the others saved by Victor get past you?"

"Guys, guys, it's only one match," Victor said.

As captain, he wanted to stop the argument from getting out of hand.

Coach Bridge gathered them together. "Well, Gazelles," he said, "you've tasted victory and you've tasted defeat. You know what both feel like now. That gives you a sense of what's ahead over the next five matches."

Victor caught up with Abbas as they were heading back to the main building. "You played really well."

"Thanks, Victor. You made some great saves. What's your school like?"

"Haunted. It's that old."

Abbas chuckled.

"That's the building," continued Victor. "The culture is, well, many cultures."

As Victor spoke, he missed Ozzie. He missed eating roti with him on Friday nights. His home life seemed so far away.

"Same here," said Abbas. "My soccer team has players from the Philippines, El Salvador, First Nations, Liberia, Congo —"

"No white players?"

"We have to let a few play," Abbas grinned.

"Feels different now it's just us Syrians," Victor said.

"Yes. A week where only soccer exists. And peace reigns. And refugees relive past memories."

"The way the old folks relive their youth."

The old — Grampa —

"Enough of this," Abbas said, jolting Victor from

his thoughts. "I hear your team is going up Grouse Mountain this afternoon. Enjoy the heights, Victor."

Amena, Sandra and Lilith escorted the Gazelles on a Skyride cable-car trip up Grouse Mountain. Victor was glad that he had listened to Amena when she said to dress warmer than usual. The cable car swayed on the way up, above snow-covered trees. Victor closed his eyes and hoped that the cables would not snap. He imagined his parents watching on TV.

Breaking News. In Vancouver this afternoon several Syrian teenagers plunged to their deaths on Grouse Mountain. And now to the weather, Heather . . .

The cable car stopped and they waited for the others to arrive. The wintry air was clean and pine-scented. He did not mind this brief return to winter. Spring was literally a drop away.

Spread out below was Vancouver's mainland in clear sunshine. To cap it off they were treated to hot chocolate, hot tea and BeaverTails pastries at Grizzly Lookout Café.

The ride back down was more fun for Victor. He was able to appreciate the tall pines. Skiers flew past them zig-zagging. There were even snowshoers weaving between the trees.

The Gazelles returned to NSDC in time for supper and an extra-early night's sleep.

Tomorrow would be a double header.

12
Double Header

Victor awoke refreshed. The pure oxygen from the top of Grouse Mountain had helped him sleep deeply. He was ready for their busiest soccer day in the schedule. Victor checked the team rosters for the day's double header. He noticed that the coaches were both women.

Round #3
9:00–10:30
GTA Gazelles vs. Regina Aleppos

Lunch
11:00–12:30

Round #4
2:00–3:30
GTA Gazelles vs. Winnipeg Green Stars

The first match started. Victor punted the ball to the middle of the field. Habib and Muta had fallen back in position to receive it. Habib trapped the ball and passed it to Muta. They turned and rushed the Aleppos defence. Muta dribbled the ball and bolted by their sweeper. Then he passed it across to Habib, who passed it back to him.

"Take the shot," Victor said under his breath. He rose up on his toes to see even better.

Muta reacted like he had heard Victor. He shot the ball. But the Aleppos goalkeeper must have also been a mind reader. He lunged across to his left, catching the ball with ease and grace. Victor watched as the goalkeeper casually rolled the ball to a nearby defender. The Aleppos took their time dribbling the ball. Victor thought they seemed confident, to the point of being cocky.

Victor saved the attack when it came. Aiming high, he tipped the ball backward with both gloved hands. Once more he punted the ball toward the centre of the field. That was the see-saw rhythm of the first scoreless half.

During halftime break the Gazelles sipped water. They munched on apples and blood oranges that came all the way from China. Coach Bridge praised the Gazelles first before getting to his other notes.

"Victor, lay off the punting in the second half. They're expecting it now and will mark our forwards even more," Coach Bridge said. "Like I might have mentioned before, good communication all round, guys. Another thing, if Firas has the ball and many of you are calling his name at once, Firas gets confused. Who to pass to? So, decide quickly if you're safe to receive the ball. Call out then."

"Safe here, Firas," Muta called out.

"That's right," Coach Bridge smiled. "Observations?"

"Regina Aleppos are dribbling way more than passing. Let's take advantage of that. Attack them more without getting yellow carded, if you can," Victor said.

A yellow card removed a player from the field for two minutes.

"Right. We can't afford too many warnings and yellow cards," Coach Bridge stated.

And that's what they stuck to. But try as they might, neither team managed to score. The match ended in a draw of 0–0.

⚽ ⚽ ⚽

Rest. Lunch. Rest.

There was a cool breeze when they took to the field. The Winnipeg Green Stars were dressed in, yes, green. Their jerseys had the same green stars as on the Syrian flag.

Victor led the Gazelles as they shouted in unison, "Great, Team, Attitude!"

Victor's reading of the first thirty-five minutes was two teams evenly matched in strength, skill and vitality.

By the end of the first half they had traded goals. One for you. One for me. One for you. One for me. The score was 2–2. Habib was the only Gazelle scorer.

"Hayyan, Malik, both of you are taking too much time with throw-ins," Coach Bridge said at halftime. "If the ball goes over the sideline and you get to throw it in, find someone quickly. The longer you take, the more time you give your opposition to get organized."

Victor decided there was only one thing to do to change the outcome. He shared with his team the secret tactic of Double Speed. When his school team had been playing against Ozzie and his Nigerian friends, Ozzie United had used it against Victor United. And Hall United, when they combined forces, had used it against the Kingston Bluffers.

"Double Speed can be used by the defence to frustrate the other team. Or it can be used by the offence to weaken them enough to score goals," Victor said, pausing. "But it is like a — a sword with both edges. Because the team using it can be weakened as well."

"We're taking a big risk," Raja spoke up. "It might be foolish to try it."

"At this point we need goals if we want to win," Coach Bridge said. He turned to Victor. "Your idea, captain. Your call."

"We have two fresh players. Bassel is replacing Anwar. Joram is replacing Hayyan," Victor said. "Hey, we're named after gazelles, right? Gazelles are fast. I call Offensive Double Speed."

"Coach, keep Anwar in as sweeper," Raja said. "I'll step out."

Victor knew that Anwar, the right defender in the diamond shape, didn't have much experience as a sweeper. But could he surprise them?

"Guys, think of—" Victor paused, hoping he would pronounce the word he was thinking of correctly, "—decathletes. Two days. Ten events. The last one is a 1600 metre run. Today, we have thirty-five more minutes. Tomorrow is a day off to recover. This is like a 1600 metre race," exclaimed Victor.

Allah, I hope this works, they're depending on me, he thought as he took his position in goal.

Thirty-five minutes seemed to go by faster than it ever had. Victor was sure Raja was wishing he was part of the thrilling second half.

Firas scored. *Bam!*

Habib scored. *Bam!* He completed a hat trick.

Muta scored. *Bam!*

The final score was 5–2.

Coach Bridge is like a teenager on a roller coaster, Victor observed. He was elated that the Double Speed tactic had worked in their favour. *I can't wait to tell Ozzie about today.*

"Good call, captain," Raja said.

Victor nodded to him. He saw that Raja regretted not being a part of the success.

Double Header

Swimming was scheduled for two teams at a time at the UBC pool. That afternoon it was the Gazelles and Montreal Gold Hawks. The teams had not yet played against each other in the tournament. Victor had met some of their players at meals.

The pool was divided down the middle. One side was for continuous swim in lanes. The other side was for games and fun activities. The lanes were longer than those at Malvern Community Centre. Victor found the water was cool and refreshing. He loved swimming. The past winter he had been too busy with soccer to enjoy a swim. He moved through the water slowly and smoothly, while others frolicked in the shallow end of the other side, tossing around a water polo ball.

Victor emptied his mind until it was clear as water. Whenever thoughts entered his head he simply let them flow out. *Mom. Dad. Gabriel. School. Ozzie. Leelah. Teammates. Coach. Gabriel. Ball. Sun. Raja. Grouse Mountain. Mountain. Grampa. Gabriel. Grampa. Breathing. Water.*

He swam under the divider into the recreational area. The activity from the others had stirred up the water into little waves. He rolled onto his back and floated, letting the water carry him wherever it wished.

13
Dolphin Blues

Victor remembered Principal Arsenault's suggestion that he try to get to Stanley Park. He ended up going in a group made up of Gazelles, Halifax Sandpipers and Winnipeg Green Stars. Some went to the Vancouver Aquarium at the heart of the park. Abbas and Victor rented bikes. At the entrance Victor bent his head backwards to take in the images on the super tall totem poles.

Abbas was the ideal guide. He had explored the park with his friends. Their aim was to bike around the entire park. Sometimes they rode side by side, other times in single file. The air was scented with early spring flowers. Victor could also smell the rich earth. Birds sang to each other. Some areas were hilly with steep descents. Victor got glimpses of the bay through the trees. Light bounced off the water.

Victor and Abbas talked about escaping Syria. They told their own stories and the stories they heard from other players.

"Poor Lasar. He lost his mother and sister in the

Mediterranean Sea so close to Turkey," Abbas said.

Victor knew that Abbas had lost his father and older brothers that way too. He thought he should let Abbas decide if he wanted to talk about that. "We heard that route gave only a fifty-fifty chance of getting across. The boats were always too full," Victor said.

"People were desperate. There was no going back," Abbas said sadly.

They rode along the Seawall with the water on one side, hugging the hillside on the other.

"In Lebanon, we were helped by a family," said Victor. "The Simons."

"Muslims?" Abbas asked.

"No, Christians. They treated us like family."

"You were lucky, then."

"Yeah, I guess."

Victor wondered if he should mention Grampa to Abbas.

They returned the bikes and hiked toward the aquarium, munching on lunches packed by the Soccer Centre's catering staff. The long entrance line moved quickly. Soon they were inside with the others.

For Victor, the most thrilling part of the aquarium was being nose to nose with a dolphin. He looked at her eyes through the thick glass. He felt like she knew him, like she was telling him something. He did not hear words, but he felt his heart opening wider and wider in his chest. And he could not stop grinning.

Tournament Fugee

❀ ❀ ❀

Victor called home before supper. Mom and Dad sounded upbeat. But he sensed there was something they were not saying.

"Yes, they're feeding us well, Mom," Victor assured her. "Put Dad on again."

"I love you, honey."

"I love you, too, Mom."

There was a pause before Dad came on the line.

"Dad, what's Mom not telling me?"

"Gabriel has double pneumonia. His system was quite weak. But he's getting the best care."

"I thought he was getting better," Victor said.

"He'sonstrongermedicationnow.He'llbefeelingbetter in no time. We have to go now. Don't worry, son. Bye."

Victor turned off the phone. "Double pneumonia? I thought pneumonia was bad," he said to no one in particular.

Abbas passed by at that moment.

"What do you know about double pneumonia, Abbas?" Victor asked.

"Is there such a thing? I've only heard about pneumonia. And I know it's pretty serious."

Victor told Abbas about Gabriel. "They keep telling me not to worry. But that's exactly what I do. I couldn't bear to lose my brother." He remembered Abbas's loss. It was too late.

Abbas saw the horrified look on Victor's face. "I'm okay about it, Victor," he said. "Everyone's had some kind of loss. But your brother's in a Canadian hospital. He'll have good care."

"That's where it went from pneumonia to double pneumonia."

They walked together to supper. Victor ate mainly to keep his energy up. Before he went to sleep he made two quick sketches of the dolphin he had seen at the aquarium. Sleep came, but soon he was wide awake again. He tossed from side to side. He couldn't stop thinking about Grampa and Gabriel. *Is Grampa angry with me because I didn't tell Abbas about him? Is Gabriel dying?*

Eventually, he fell into a short sleep.

The remaining three matches were scheduled in the mornings with afternoons free.

Round #5
9:00–10:30
GTA Gazelles vs Halifax Sandpipers

"No, I don't need help with that," Victor snapped at Dani during halftime. The match against the Halifax Sandpipers was not going well for the Gazelles. They were being outplayed with tremendous skill on every line. The score was 1–3. Dani had managed the lone goal for the Gazelles.

What's my defence doing? Victor asked himself. *What am I doing?*

"You have thirty-five minutes to get back in the match. Possession. Possession. Possession," Coach Bridge emphasized.

Coach Bridge handed Victor a bottle of juice. The only thing he said was, "Keep alert."

The second half did not start much better. Then Habib found his form and scored twice. But the last goal was not allowed because he had been offside, so the final score was 2–4.

When they were shaking hands with the Halifax Sandpipers, Victor noticed Raja shaking his head at him.

"I'm sorry," said Victor to his team. "I feel like I've let you down."

"Everyone has a bad day, sometimes," Dani said coming to his defence.

While everyone scattered, Raja muttered, "Only weak goalkeepers need to say they're sorry."

Victor felt like punching him. Coach Bridge could see his anger. He told Victor he wanted to meet with him after lunch. Victor walked away. It was the mature thing to do. He looked back in time to see Coach Bridge and Raja laughing. *Are they laughing at me?*

During lunch Victor recapped the tournament so far: Win, loss, draw, win, loss. Not great. He decided that

Coach Bridge was likely going to replace him as goalkeeper with Raja. And then Raja would be captain also.

Victor headed to the dorm room. No one else was there. He started packing his suitcase.

Victor debated with himself. "I'll speak first. No, I'll hear what Coach has to say. No, I'll go first. I'll tell him to replace me with Raja and send me home. Then I can be with Gabriel," he said aloud.

At Coach Bridge's suggestion they walked through UBC Botanical Garden. The sky was overcast but the sun peeked through the clouds. Coach Bridge began speaking before Victor could say anything.

"I had a wife in Syria," Coach Bridge said. "We divorced. No children. She remarried. Some of my friends ended up dead. Martyrs. For what? When the troubles got worse, I had no reason to stay."

Victor did not know if he wanted a response.

"We are not the first people to leave a homeland by force, Victor. And we must not feel guilty for getting away and for surviving while others perished."

Victor thought that Coach Bridge was still feeling some kind of guilt despite his words. Maybe that's what drove him to be part of the tournament. He needed to find some purpose for continuing.

"Victor, you're a terrific goalkeeper. You think quickly on your feet. You anticipate an opponent's moves. You've inspired the team. They trust you. That match against Regina — nil–nil. Flawless."

Victor listened, surprised. He still wanted to say that he should be replaced as captain, but the words could not come out.

"Today, your energy and your focus — they were not there. What happened?"

"I didn't sleep well."

"It happens. Not every day will be flawless. Don't expect it," Coach Bridge said. "You've adjusted to this new life. You've found a passion in soccer. Keep that. Let it carry you to other things."

"My brother has double pneumonia," Victor blurted out. "I found out yesterday."

They stopped walking. Coach Bridge looked at Victor. "That kind of news is a lot to carry around, even for an adult."

Victor told him the whole story, starting with taking Gabriel tobogganing.

"He's getting the care that he needs, Victor. I'm glad you told me. I've noticed that you are kind and show concern for others. They call that compassion. It's a good thing. If you want to talk more, I'm available anytime, day or night. Okay?"

"Okay, Coach."

Victor felt a little better about Gabriel. But Grampa's death still weighed on his mind. He spent a long time alone in the prayer room. He did not sketch anything that day.

In bed, he dozed off easily and slept for ten hours straight.

14
Stories We Tell

Victor was watching a highlight reel of Wayne Greenish, along with the other seven tournament captains. After the applause ended, the soccer star sat with them in a circle.

"This workshop is about you, leaders." Wayne Greenish looked around at each of them. "I've watched all your teams so far, even if it was just portions of matches. I'm impressed with your talent. Yes, you too, St. John's Euphrates," he said, winking at the captain from his hometown.

"The role of captain, as leader, is a flexible one," Greenish continued. "It changes from age level to age level, from national matches to international ones. And at each level the pressure is different. So, what makes a good leader?"

One by one hands shot up.

"One who thinks clearly."

"A good listener to teammates."

"Someone who cares about the team."

"Admits mistakes."

"Understands the game completely and can help the team because of that," Victor said.

"Yes, mastery," Wayne Greenish agreed. "What else?"

"Works harder than his teammates."

"Has a sense of responsibility."

"Let's stop there. No wrong answers, really. For the purpose of this workshop we'll focus on responsibility."

Wayne Greenish organized two groups of four. The captains shared examples of how they had acted with responsibility on and off the field. Victor learned a lot. But he avoided sharing that he had not been responsible enough about Gabriel.

"Don't be afraid of making decisions — quick decisions, hard decisions," Wayne Greenish advised. Then he sent them off to their morning matches with a final note. "As captains, leaders, yours is not the only perspective on the field. You have a team with other thoughts and ideas you can use, whether you all agree or not. Teamwork. There's nothing like it. Keep studying this game. What you learn will apply whether you lead a high school team, an MLS team, a retail store, a marketing department or even a country. And like we say in Newfoundland, 'long may your big jib draw.' That means 'May you have good fortune for a long, long time!'"

Then he shook each of them by the hand.

⚽ ⚽ ⚽

Round #6
9:00–10:30
GTA Gazelles vs. St. John's Euphrates

During the warm-up for the match against the St. John's Euphrates, Habib complained of a headache. Victor told Coach Bridge. He thought about the leaders workshop from just twenty minutes before. So he took quick action and asked Amena to fetch one of the medics who were on stand-by for the players. Habib was given a pill for the pain and escorted to his room to rest.

"Joram will replace Habib for the first half. We'll see how Habib feels at halftime," Coach Bridge announced to the team.

Victor knew that Habib was being taken care of. But Habib was a key player and their top scorer. Joram had always subbed in the second half. How would he be as a starter?

The St. John's Euphrates team was from Newfoundland and Labrador on the east coast. They started off strong, like the mighty currents of the Syrian river they were named after. Joram and Muta took a while to get a rhythm of passing going. It was clear to Victor that both defences were strong. Both he and the Euphrates goalkeeper saved or deflected the shots to their goals.

By halftime they were scoreless: 0–0. Coach Bridge consulted with Victor. "Habib's headache has eased a lot," Coach Bridge told him.

"That's good news, Coach," Victor said, gulping some water.

"I want Joram to continue."

"He's playing well with Muta, I admit. But he hasn't played a full match with us," Victor argued.

"Do you believe in Joram's skills?"

Victor thought about that. The leaders workshop was fresh in his brain. "Yeah — of course."

"Then we let Habib rest. He's contributed a lot to the team already. We'll need him fresh for our last match tomorrow."

Victor nodded. But he hoped they would do better than another draw. He did not have to wait long to find out.

Victor watched the ball. He saw a pair of familiar feet dribbling the ball. Other, opposing feet chased. The Gazelles feet moved to the right with speed and lightness. The right foot stopped the ball. The Euphrates feet moved past, unable to stop. The Gazelles foot kicked the ball up, over to a teammate. The new Gazelles feet ran past the Euphrates feet with triple speed. Then they stopped and the right foot trapped the ball to control it and fired it into the net.

A huge grin appeared on Victor's face as his teammates mobbed a happy Joram, who had scored his first goal of the tournament.

Victor's confidence soared. He saw everything with a clearer head. He directed his teammates, anticipating the moves of Euphrates forwards and midfielders. After all, he had studied them during the first half.

"Raja, watch out for that striker!" he shouted.

"Yes, boss."

Malik scored next. Hayyan headed in one more with seconds to spare before the final whistle blew. The final score was 3–0. The Gazelles produced a solid blanking, the scoring all done by three players who had not scored before in the tournament.

"Great, Team, Attitude!" they shouted in unison.

Raja was the first to start high-fiving the team — including Victor.

Can we do this again? Victor wondered.

"Guys, we're now tied with Montreal Gold Hawks in points," Coach Bridge said. "We're doing very well. Better than I had hoped. If we win tomorrow, we get to play in the final. Do you want one more match or two?"

"Two!" they all shouted.

"Then you must dig even deeper. You must focus and play your best. Ask yourself, each of you, 'Have I played my best soccer?'"

The Gazelles were suddenly hungry to be the eastern finalists. During lunch Victor overheard players say that Montreal might take the whole tournament.

Others were saying Vancouver. Nobody was saying GTA Gazelles.

Victor took some lunch to Habib and gave him the good news.

"You really think we have a chance, Victor?" asked Habib.

"Hard to say, Habib. Actually, yes, we have a chance. But it can't be a draw, we have to beat them. That's why I want you to take it easy for the rest of the day."

"I thought it was Coach who wanted me to rest more."

"Well, we both decided that."

"Okay, captain," Habib said, smiling. "I'll take your advice. Thanks for lunch."

"No problem." Victor bumped fists with him.

As he headed to the showers, Victor thought of how he had changed since the school year had started. All of the taunts from Raja would have made that Victor react with his fists. That was what had happened when he and Ozzie, with their own teams, fought over the use of the school's field. It led to the Victor United and Ozzie United match in front of the school. Then members of both teams formed Hall United and played a friendly match against the Division Champions Kingston Bluffers. After that match, the Bluffers coach, Coach Jeong-Hough, invited Victor and Ozzie as co-goalkeepers on her new indoor league Scarborough Tigers. The idea that it all had started with a fight brought a smile to his face.

The team headed out that afternoon. Amena, Sandra and Lilith escorted the Gazelles and the Regina Aleppos and their guides to the Nitobe Memorial Garden. In the Japanese garden, Victor marvelled at the trees, shrubs, waterfalls and stone lanterns. He looked into the reflecting pond at the koi swimming.

"The garden is in memory of a man who wanted to bring together the people of Japan and Canada," Lilith informed them.

Victor thought of Grampa. Who would remember him? There was nothing to mark his grave beside a lonely highway in Syria. Victor picked up a flat grey stone and secretly wrote Grampa's name on it with the sketching pencil he always carried. Then he placed it beside a stream where the water would wash away the pencil mark.

That evening Victor drew a section of the garden with a bridge and a stone lantern. On a tree he wrote the name Bayazid.

Outside rain thundered. Victor remembered that their next game would be on the grass of Field #4. Would a soaking wet grass field make them delay or cancel the matches? He was lulled to sleep by the rhythm of rain tapping against the window.

15
Elimination Time

Round #7
9:00–10:30
GTA Gazelles vs. Montreal Gold Hawks

Sometimes an elimination match is played with wild desperation. Victor had seen it on TV. And he had experienced it with the Scarborough Tigers.

Round #7 started out with the sun high in the sky. But the sun was not strong enough to bake the field dry. Habib was back in the line-up. But the Montreal Gold Hawks played rougher than the teams the Gazelles had played before. There was a lot of slipping and sliding in the mud. Victor thought it looked more like a rugby match.

Two Gold Hawks midfielders received cautions at the same time and had to sit out for two minutes. The Gazelles leaped on the opportunity. Muta scored the first goal, giving them a halftime lead of 1–0.

But Gold Hawks didn't give up easily in the second

half. Raja slid the ball to an opposing forward by accident, causing the forward to score on a blocked Victor. The score was tied 1–1.

"Don't worry, Raja. We'll recover quickly," Victor said.

"Okay," Raja replied, but he seemed rattled.

Habib scored, proving Victor right and making it 2–1. The final ten minutes was all defence for the Gazelles. Raja was in fine form. They held on, denying the Gold Hawks an equalizer or a winning goal.

The Gazelles were celebrating, even though they looked and felt beat-up.

"Thanks for not yelling at me in front of the team, Victor," Raja whispered. "I hate messing up."

Victor looked at Raja and realized that his weakness was his fear *of* making mistakes. "Everyone messes up sometimes, Raja. You recovered well," he whispered back.

"Team, well done," said Coach Bridge. "I've decided not to hold a practice tomorrow. It's your scheduled free day. You deserve to have it off. We'll have Saturday morning to practice."

Right then, he got a phone call. The western finalists were no big surprise — the Vancouver Herons. The Gazelles would be playing the home team in the final on Saturday.

After lunch the Gazelles were taken to North Vancouver, called North Van. At the Capilano

Suspension Bridge, they had to wait for a wedding couple ahead of them who were having their pictures taken.

"Don't look down or you'll want to jump over," Johnny teased his teammates.

Victor walked across the bridge, holding the cables, arms outstretched. He summoned his courage to look down at the river far, far below. He wondered if the people who made the bridge felt like they were making a link to the edge of the world. As most of the Gazelles also braved the cliff-walk, Victor overheard some cruise ship tourists say they were heading to Alaska next. *Okay, that's the new edge of the world,* he thought.

When they returned to NSDC Victor phoned Ozzie. "How was the cross-country skiing in Barrie?" Victor asked.

"Plenty of snow, as usual. I'm going to try out for the national team next year. But only if I can kick the ball while I ski," Ozzie said laughing.

"Cross-country winter soccer. I get it."

"Or even better, ice-skating soccer."

"We could start a league," Victor suggested. "But first we'd have to learn to skate."

"Who needs to learn to skate? Let's slide and fall all over the arena like clowns. More entertaining for the spectators," Ozzie suggested.

It felt good to be laughing with his friend.

"So, how's the tournament going?" Ozzie asked.

"Believe it or not . . ."

". . . Okay, I won't believe it . . ."

"We're in the final on Saturday."

"And who says there's no Allah! That's great news. When were you going to tell me?"

"I just did."

"But I had to ask. That should have been the first thing out of your mouth."

Victor told Ozzie about meeting Abbas again after years. He shared his use of Double Speed against the Winnipeg Green Stars. He talked about the leadership workshop and the trips to Stanley Park and Grouse Mountain. He even told Ozzie about his sketches.

⚽ ⚽ ⚽

The next day, while the Herons held a practice, the Gazelles and several other "brothers" visited the Museum of Anthropology. They posed for pictures beside the giant totem poles. Amena told them that it was the first day of the annual Coastal First Nations Dance Festival.

Inside, Victor was transported with laughter by a dance performance that had comedic characters. As an encore, the show's narrator stepped closer to the audience, now in the role of storyteller. She greeted the adults. Then she greeted the children. She beat her drum and then introduced a story about two young birds, who were sisters. She beat her drum some more and continued.

"The older bird. Always the older one, eh?" said the storyteller. "She dared her sister to fly off a mountain. The bird flew off, but her wings were not yet developed. The younger sister crashed into the forest below. And died. The older sister, she was not sure of the strength of her wings. She decided not to follow. Let me tell you, she felt guilty and heartbroken. She could not forgive herself for causing her sister's death. Years later — well, bird years later — that older sister grew up. She became strong and good at flying. She soared and landed softer than airplanes at Vancouver International Airport — fog or no fog. She became wise. She learned that at each moment you make a choice that you alone are responsible for. She forgave herself. And she healed."

Returning to the NSDC, Victor met up with Abbas. He did not talk about his practice. And they avoided talking about the final match. Walking along a path, Victor thought about the story he had just heard. He told Abbas about the day he and his family stopped along the highway.

"I kicked the ball toward Gabriel without stopping it first. The spinning ball rolled onto the middle of the highway. Without thinking, I went to get it. Grampa was shouting something so I stopped in the middle of the road. The next thing I knew Grampa pushed me. I wondered why he did that. I looked back when I heard the horn of a truck blaring. Grampa had picked up the ball. Abbas, there was this look on his face a second before —"

Tears welled up in Victor's eyes. But he had to finish. He owed that to Grampa.

"We buried him along the highway. We could not put up a marker with his name. The authorities would have known we had fled and in which direction. We had to keep the Bayazid name safe."

"Wow," said Abbas. It was almost a whisper.

"My fault," said Victor.

"An accident, Victor," Abbas said.

"My fault, still."

"Thanks for sharing that with me. I know how hard it is to tell people about losing your family."

"Thank you for listening without telling me how to feel."

They parted and Victor went to his prayer room for some quiet time before supper.

16
To the Final Match

By the time the GTA Gazelles entered BC Place Stadium late Saturday morning all the other teams were already there in the audience. The day before, the teams that didn't make the final were allowed twenty-minute mini matches to get a taste of the big field, a sort of consolation gift. The Vancouver Herons were finishing their practice. Soon the field would be free for the Gazelles to have their practice.

The Gazelles entered at field level. Their eyes bulged. Their jaws dropped. Their heads turned 360 degrees to take in the cavernous stadium. They were rendered speechless. As soccer players, they were in a holy of holies. It came close to, but also very different from, Victor's experience entering the magnificent Great Mosque of Damascus as a child.

How did he get there? If anyone had told him at the start of the school year that he was going to be playing on this field on this day, he would have said, "No way!"

To the Final Match

The Gazelles began an hour-long practice to get a feel for the largest field of their playing lives. Coach Bridge took them through strategies they had talked about at the NSDC. He reminded them of the Herons tactics from the game against the Gazelles exactly a week before. They had to keep in mind that their opponents might or might not change some of those tactics.

"So you've played them before," said Coach Bridge. "Don't underestimate them. You know where their offence is strongest, their striker."

"Abbas," Victor offered.

"Finally the *intelligence* I asked for a week ago," Dani teased.

"Be determined and focused. But be flexible with your approaches," Coach Bridge said. "Today, this field is your home. Be comfortable here."

Victor handled the practice shots on goal as best he could. He looked on silently as Coach Bridge had Raja and Bassel, as backup goalkeepers, receive practice shots on goal also. Victor hoped that he did not break an ankle or have an injury and have to leave the game. He had come this far. He needed to complete this tournament with his team.

Victor looked up as the retractable roof began to open and sunlight streamed onto the field. With practice over, the Gazelles got a tour of the complex. While the guide talked about the stadium which was opened in 1983 and renovated in 2009 for use during the 2010 Winter Olympics, Victor's mind went to Gabriel. Gabriel would be amazed to see this place. Victor wondered how Gabriel was doing. But he decided not to call Mom and Dad. If there was any news they would call him. That was their promise the night before when he told them that he would be playing in the final. Still, he began to feel anxious. He was not sure if it was being in such a big stadium or if he was sensing something about Gabriel's condition. *Children do die from pneumonia*, he thought. *Double pneumonia, surely*.

From high in the stands, Victor saw the *W* for Vancouver Whitecaps FC at centre field. He hoped it stood for *winning* for the Gazelles as well.

During lunch in the food court, Victor decided he needed to pay attention to his teammates. "I'm here for those who can't be. I'll call Mom and Dad after the match," he whispered to himself.

Raja appeared beside him. They were both silent for a moment. Then Raja said quietly, "I heard that your brother is in the hospital, Victor. How's he doing?"

Victor was surprised by Raja's concern. "He's — he's getting better." Victor didn't want to go into details. "Thanks for asking."

Raja nodded. Then he was gone so quickly that Victor questioned if it had really happened.

To the Final Match

After lunch both teams relaxed in the Pitchside Club Lounge. Victor and Abbas avoided each other until it was time to head to their separate locker rooms.

"You nervous?" Victor asked Abbas.

"Kind of," Abbas replied. "You?"

"Just another away match," Victor shrugged.

"Not really, my friend, not really," Abbas chuckled. "See you out there."

"I'll see you first," Victor said.

And they bumped fists.

Before the Gazelles left the locker room, Victor gathered them together. "Each of us knows why we chose to come to this tournament. We made that choice — as individuals. But we're here together. We're going out there as a team. Together. We're brothers on and off that field."

Victor noticed Raja drop his head down.

"Let's show Canada our talents as we give thanks. Together," Victor concluded.

"Together," his teammates responded without any prompting.

"One more time," Victor said and they joined him in a circle.

"Great! Team! Attitude!"

Victor was surprised by his own burst of emotion. He had not planned to give a speech.

All the Gazelles were silent, in their own thoughts, as they filed out of the locker room.

Nothing in the world could have prepared the Gazelles and the Herons for the roar of 54,500 screaming children and youths as they arrived on the field. The other six teams were introduced from their section in the stands and also received a rousing welcome.

A Syrian girl, wearing a simple orange hijab and showing her full face, began a passionate rendition of "O Canada." Victor felt a tingling up his spine. He felt a wave of belonging wash over him. All the refugees were no longer immigrants. They were Canadian.

If only Grampa was alive and here to share this . . .

He shook off the thought.

"I have always asked you to do your best," Coach Bridge began. "In order to do your best you must feel good about yourself. Three words, guys: Communication. Flexibility. Fun."

Kickoff began promptly at one o'clock. Muta won the coin toss. Victor was aware that in previous games the Gazelles forwards had been slow off the mark. But today Habib wasted no time. Receiving the ball back from Muta, he crossed it over to Hayyan. He dribbled and passed to Firas. They all pushed toward the Herons defence. Habib waved for the ball, received it and dribbled past one defender and another. He faked the goalkeeper, sending him to his right and tapped the ball to his left into the net. The Gazelles were ahead 1–0.

Victor had never seen Habib so charged. He looked up at the electronic score clock while the Gazelles celebrated. Fifty-eight seconds. "That must be some kind of record for one of the fastest goals," Victor said to himself.

The Herons controlled the speed of play with their kickoff. They doubled the mark on Habib. He was now a serious threat to them. The Herons quickly gained a corner kick and converted it to a clean, successful header by Samir. 1–1.

The Vancouver spectators cheered and hollered. Then they started chanting:

H-E-R-O-N-S!
Herons! Herons! Herons! Herons!

The Gazelles had a kickoff once more. Before they could use a tactic, Abbas stole the ball and bolted past the Gazelles defence. He got a cannon of a shot past Victor. The Herons were ahead 1–2.

Abbas grinned at Victor, who returned his smile. Abbas had beaten him, no contest.

Victor managed two more saves before the halftime whistle.

Coach Bridge addressed the team at the break. "Guys, you proved you can score against them. Score again. Every chance you get, take the shot. Take it. And if it does not go into the net right away, prepare for rebounds."

"Some of you may be thinking, 'We're losing,'" he continued. "You are not losing because you are behind by one goal. You have not figured out how to beat this team — yet. Go back out there —" He paused and Victor saw that tears were falling down his cheeks. Coach Bridge wiped his face with both hands. He did not apologize as he said, "Go out there with Syrian pride. Go out there with Canadian joy in your hearts. Play safe. Play strong."

Victor wondered why he did not say, "Play to win." *Maybe he forgot,* Victor thought. *Maybe he does not think we can win.*

17
The Second Half

Dani was a solid midfielder. He had scored goals during the tournament. Victor knew Dani made every effort to follow Coach Bridge's and Victor's advice and instructions.

Dani had a determined look on his face when he received a pass from Hayyan. Dani dribbled, faked, reversed and drove forward again. He treated the Herons defence like they were invisible. Facing the goalkeeper, he faked to the left, then faked to the right, then faked to the left once more. He shot the ball with his other foot. It was totally unexpected. Even Victor was not sure what he was seeing. He didn't know how a goalkeeper could face a play like that. Dani made the equalizer. The score was tied 2–2.

With his arms open wide, Dani ran toward his excited teammates. Sometimes gut instinct ruled, Victor realized. What Dani had done was not pre-planned. The worst thing that might have happened was loss of possession. He had gambled the way Victor had with Double Speed against the Regina Aleppos.

The crowd chanted and chanted. He was not sure anymore who they were chanting for, the home team or the eastern visitors — or both.

It seemed like the Herons thought, "Why not us?" They returned the attack. Their left midfielder scored against Victor with a reverse scissor kick that no one saw coming. Not Johnny, not Raja, not Victor. The Herons were ahead again, 2–3.

Victor passed the word from his defenders to midfielders to Habib and Muta: "Dig deeper."

With regulation time running out Victor saved two more attacks to his goal. And then there were 110 seconds to go. It was that magical twilight in soccer when the lagging team could produce an equalizer. Or the leading team could score one more goal to prevent it. All of this swirled like a whirlpool in Victor's brain. This would be when heroes were born.

Who would it be? he thought. *A forward? Perhaps. A midfielder? Perhaps. A defender? Not likely. Not unless all players stormed the opposition.*

Joram secured a corner kick. He did not have much practice with corners and he quickly mentioned this to Victor. Together, they selected Dani to take the shot. Joram joined the mix in front of the Herons goal. And, so, with seconds ticking toward a Herons victory, Dani kicked the ball. The ball moved with the right speed at the right height with the right curve. It sailed, no, it floated straight to Joram's head. As it touched his head, Joram turned it one micro degree into the Herons net.

And — the whistle blew.

It was the end of regulation time.

The score was 3–3.

They would have a penalty shootout to decide the game.

Victor and Coach Bridge picked Habib, Muta, Firas, Hayyan and Dani to shoot, in that order. The Herons picks were, in order, Abbas, Daniel, Nabil, Gabriel and Samir. Samir had scored against Victor with the reverse scissor kick. It was up to Victor and the Herons goalkeeper Muhammad to try to stop the alternating strikers.

All 54,500 spectators clapped and hollered on their feet. They were, after all, the home crowd. Their team was on the verge of victory.

Coach Bridge took Victor aside. "Nothing matters anymore, Victor," he said calmly. "Not the stadium, not the tournament, not the team. Not even Raja."

In that moment Victor realized that Coach Bridge knew all along. He had seen Raja's attitude toward him.

Coach Bridge continued. "The next few minutes will be about you receiving a gift from Allah, the gift of a beautiful ball five times. And each time you must embrace the gift and be thankful."

It was not easy but Victor managed to blank out everything in his head. He focused on each second. He saw Raja turn away, not wanting to look at the shots. *At least he's not looking at me in judgement*, Victor thought.

Abbas shot the ball toward Victor's upper left corner. Victor did not blink. He reached up and spread both hands. He pushed the ball away, rather than letting it come into his gloves. No goal.

Habib's shot rolled low, but it was fast. Too fast for the Herons goalkeeper. Muhammad's dive was too slow. Goal.

Daniel was next. The ball went straight into Victor's hands. No goal.

Muta's shot hit the left post and bounced outside of the net. No goal.

Nabil's shot went to Victor's upper right corner. It struck the joint of the frame and bounced over the line. Goal.

Firas sent the ball low left at Muhammad's goal, hard. Goal.

Gabriel sent it at Victor's shoulder level. Victor reacted too late. Goal.

Hayyan scored for the Gazelles.

Samir was too fast for Victor and scored.

So far, the Herons had scored 3. With only Dani left to kick, the Gazelles had scored 3 as well. If Dani scored, victory was theirs. If not, they would select additional players to kick.

Dani had analyzed goalkeeper Muhammad through the two games and the shootout. He stepped back from the ball. The ref blew the whistle. Dani took three steps and shot the ball. It went low and hard, just out of reach of Muhammad.

Goal.

The stadium of children, still standing, went wild. Their team had not won, but they had witnessed a great match of a game they loved.

The Gazelles mobbed Dani. They piled on top of each other. Coach Bridge joined in their celebration of hugs and high fives.

"Great! Team! Attitude! Together! Together! Together! Together!" they chanted.

The Gazelles and Herons lined up and shook hands. Victor and Abbas added a high-five to each other.

"Friends again," Abbas said.

"Brothers again," Victor added.

"Congratulations, Victor," Abbas said.

The GTA Gazelles assembled for a group photo against a backdrop of the crowd. No one was in a hurry to leave. They were still on their feet. They chanted for all the teams. The organizers managed to get all eight teams onto the field. The chants got louder and louder.

The players could not hear each other so they stopped trying to speak. They soaked in the love they were receiving. It occurred to Victor that the children were thanking them for thanking them.

Memories for a lifetime, Victor thought.

⚽ ⚽ ⚽

When the stadium finally began to empty Victor found a quiet spot. He phoned Mom.

"Yes, yes," she said. "We saw it all on CBC, live. We were watching in Gabriel's room."

"Did he watch, too?" asked Victor.

"Of course, honey. We're so proud of you for what you've done."

But Victor did not want to talk about himself. He had a reason for calling and he needed answers. "Tell me the truth, Mom."

"It's true that Gabriel was getting worse," said Mom. "But the doctors changed the medication. Now he's much improved. Dr. Holder says he'll have a full recovery."

Dr. Holder was Ozzie's mom. Victor was glad to hear she was overseeing Gabriel's case.

"She said he was 'out of the woods,'" Mom went on. "I think she means okay."

"That's good, Mom," said Victor. "I'll see you all tomorrow. Tell Gabriel I send him a big hug. You, too. And Dad."

As Victor clicked off, he began to cry. He could not

stop himself. Tears of relief that Gabriel was definitely okay mixed with tears of joy. At the game's end he had felt so much love. Victor had held onto his emotions the way he held onto a ball after catching it. Only longer, much longer. And now he could let them go.

He dried his eyes and rejoined his teammates on the field.

"Great job, captain," said Raja, extending his hand.

Victor shook it.

"I'm glad it was you in goal and not me," Raja said with a smile.

I'm glad, too, thought Victor.

"Thanks, Raja," he said.

"You're a fine captain, Victor," said Raja. "I mean it."

And Victor could see that he did.

18
Farewell

When they returned to the NSDC it was only four o'clock. Victor felt like time had expanded and he had lived a whole day since the start of the game. In some ways, he had.

Lilith woke him from a one-hour nap in time to get ready for the farewell supper. The meal was extra special. It ended with pistachio ice cream. Instead of the players collecting their food cafeteria-style, they were served by wait staff at their tables. This time they sat with their teammates, one table per team.

The Syrian Consulate in Vancouver presented the players with this parting meal. There was no head table separating the players. Consulate staff and representatives from all levels of British Columbia's governments sat among players, coaches, organizers and volunteers. For this tournament, there were no trophies, no medals and no player-of-the-match award handed out. All players received a personalized Certificate of Participation.

Farewell

Committee member Mr. Sanders rose from his table to address the crowd. "Now that you can remember the eight Samirs, the fifteen Anwars and the thirty-seven Muhammads," he started, to huge laughter, "I urge you to maintain contact with your new brothers."

Vancouver's Mayor Waldron ended his brief speech by announcing a final treat for Sunday morning.

Their last morning in Vancouver, the Gazelles gathered in a meeting room.

"Let me say, once more, how proud I am of all of you," Coach Bridge told them. "Your dedication, your persistence, your ability to rise from defeats and to snatch victories under pressure will strengthen you for whatever you do with your lives going forward. Thank you, thank you, thank you. *As-salam Alaikum*," he said, wishing God's peace upon them.

"*Wa-laikum as-salam*," they all responded, wishing God's peace back.

The private boat sliced through the calm, early morning waters of Vancouver's harbour. Over the loudspeaker, Mayor Waldron's voice spoke of a love for his city. He pointed out key places and shared memories.

Victor held his face up to the sun and breathed in the salty air. He would miss this city. He took it all in, intending to sketch from memory. He hoped to return to explore more of its beauty and treasures.

"I hope you come back," Abbas said, reading Victor's thoughts.

"Only if you promise to come to Toronto," Victor replied.

"I'll have to get a job first and save up, *inshallah*," said Abbas, expressing his hope that Allah would make it so. "Deal."

"Deal."

They bumped fists.

At the airport later that morning, Victor thanked Amena, Sandra and Lilith on behalf of his teammates for their hospitality. There were tearful and joyful goodbyes. Bonds had been formed. Email addresses and phone numbers were exchanged.

Victor was lucky to get a window seat again for the flight. He stared out at the clouds below and remembered Coach Bridge saying, "We must not feel guilty for leaving and for surviving while others perished."

His mind flashed back to what the First Nations storyteller had said about choice. He finally saw that Grampa had made a choice. He had sacrificed himself for Victor. Victor felt grateful for that act of love and would honour Grampa for it.

Victor recalled something else the storyteller had said that he had not paid much attention to at the time: "Life is now, friends. Grab it with a hunger and a passion you never knew you had. And let the rest fall away."

"Let the rest fall away," Victor whispered to himself.

He thought of how much he had experienced during the matches, especially the last penalty shootout. He looked back at Raja, two rows behind, and realized that his teammate had been, in his way, a teacher. Raja had forced Victor to be a more responsible leader.

Victor sensed that Grampa would not want him to continue in pain, feeling badly about his death. Victor decided, there high above the clouds, to let the past fall away.

"I forgive myself," he whispered. Inside, he felt like it was spring at last.

Dad met Victor at the airport. They drove straight to the hospital where Victor reunited with Mom and Gabriel. Gabriel looked much better than when Victor had left eleven days earlier.

"I'm so happy to be with my family again," Victor cried, as if he had been on a long journey.

And he had.

EPILOGUE
Mr. Greenidge's Offer

Principal Arsenault welcomed everyone back after the March Break at an assembly in the gym. She spoke about how they could give thanks by example and not just words. She singled out students who had showed gratitude around the school. Then she asked Victor to come forward. He walked up, not shuffling, but with a strong leader's confidence.

Principal Arsenault read from a scrolled certificate: "William Hall PS Recognizes Victor Bayazid for his Efforts of Gratitude through the Wonder of Sport."

She presented the certificate to Victor. He was surprised and felt slightly embarrassed when the whole school applauded.

Victor learned at lunch that Ozzie and Muhammad had spread word of how Victor spent his March Break. Many students had watched the final match on CBC. As lunch wound up, Leelah walked by. She and Victor locked eyes briefly.

Then Mr. Greenidge stopped at his table. Victor

Mr. Greenidge's Offer

liked Mr. Greenidge. He had formed and coached Hall United in the fall.

"Victor, Ozzie, Muhammad, I'm thinking of coaching a summer league team," said Mr. Greenidge. "I'm forming a multi-racial team with players who know how to get along. Hint, hint. Let me know your plans for the summer. Otherwise, on June thirtieth, at eleven p.m., I will board Caribbean Airlines back to Tobago for the summer. I will lie on the beach every day like a tourist. I will eat fried bake 'n' shark with slices of avocado for breakfast, washed down with coconut water from a real coconut and not from a can. I will look for a pretty wife at last. And I'll forget about every single one of you." Mr. Greenidge grinned.

They grinned back.

At home, Victor thought about Mr. Greenidge's offer. He had a couple of months and could take his time deciding.

Victor replaced the sketch in the silver frame on the sideboard with a new one. It was a colourful drawing of a setting sun behind green, summery Grouse Mountain, complete with tiny Skyride cable cars. In the foreground was Grampa, radiant and smiling broadly, holding a bright red, yellow and orange soccer ball.

Acknowledgements

Once again, a huge thank you to my talented editor, Kat Mototsune, for clarity and perspective. Thanks to visionary Jim and Team Lorimer. Super special thanks to Renée for enduring love.

I wish to thank my early English/Creative Writing teachers for their encouragement: Coline Gardhouse, Judith Millen, David Teddiman, Dennis Boulton, Robert Collins, Alex Bostok, Ian Waldron and professor Bob Simmons.